Fighting Chance

Kendall isn't fearless, but to get a scoop, the reporter pulls no punches, but this story takes unexpected turns that force her to stretch well beyond her reporting skills. Everything she believes about herself is challenged when she meets Chad, a stubborn fighter who takes her breath away and simultaneously sets off alarm bells in her head.

Chad is a wanted man. Champion fighters want to fight him. Women want him to love them. Major companies want to stop the small fighting operation. And a pretty and insistent reporter wants to interview him. The more she pesters, the harder he resists...

What begins as a relatively benign interview soon turns into something neither Kendall nor Chad could have anticipated. For the first time in his life, he finds himself drawn to a woman who isn't fawning all over him, and it drives him crazy.

It takes more effort than he hoped, but when a dinner leads to a night neither will soon forget. Will she let down her guard and take him at his word or is their night together the end for them?

Fighting Chance

Toni Denise

*For Jeff for putting up with my random questions throughout the
writing of this story.
I love you*

Chapter One

The conference room was so quiet, you could hear a pin drop as everyone went around the table talking about their stories they were working on. It was an intense meeting each week as everyone pitched their ideas and waited for their boss to approve them or tear them a new one.

This week, she already knew she was in trouble. The story that she had was lame, but it was the only thing she'd come up with. Why in the world had anyone thought she'd be a good fit as a sports reporter?

Robert, her boss, called on her. "Kendall?"

"I'm following the trade deal on the Badgers." Their local soccer team was trading a few players.

"No one cares. Come up with something better before tomorrow, or you're fired. I've warned you too many times that you need hard-hitting articles, and I'm not going to do it again. Be in my office first thing in the morning with a better idea or a letter of resignation—you choose which," he bellowed.

Robert didn't speak, he only yelled. It was terrifying at first, and then you got used to it. He'd fire her though. She knew he was a lot of bluster sometimes, but this was serious. She *had* been told too many times.

He moved on to the next person and approved their article before the meeting was dismissed. Everyone quickly left the conference room, a few sending her sympathetic looks as they did.

She let herself be the last one out of the room, shutting her laptop and stacking her notebook on top before picking it up and heading for her small desk on the floor with everyone else.

"What are you going to do?" Sindee, her friend and lifestyle reporter asked as she reached her desk.

"I have no idea. If I had a better story idea, I would have led with that." She dropped her head into her hands as she sat. "I'm screwed."

"You'll come up with something." She patted Kendall on the back before walking away.

"Gee, thanks," she muttered.

Kendall drew herself up and took a fortifying breath before opening her computer. She did the same thing that she always did and scoured the internet for other sports articles, looking for anything that she might be able to use as an idea for something local.

They didn't have many local teams, and their soccer team wasn't wildly popular. Though, maybe if more people read about them, they'd grow more interested.

The local university was closed for the summer, as far as sports went, so there was nothing there. No one who went there wanted to talk to her anyway.

That was her other issue: so many men who didn't want to talk to a female sports reporter. It wasn't like she was clueless, but they all assumed she was, and she'd been told more than once not to worry her pretty little head over the men things.

That always pissed her off. Her phone rang, and she answered without looking who it was, welcoming the distraction.

"Hey, kiddo," said the voice.

"Hey, Dad. What's up?"

"How's work?" He knew she'd been struggling.

"Not so great."

"Well, let me take you to lunch and see what I can do to help," he offered.

"I don't think there's much you can do to help, but I'll let you buy me lunch because I'm about to lose my job and won't have any food." She was whining, and she knew it.

"Don't talk like that. You know it will go better than that. I'll see you at the pub at noon."

"Thanks, Dad."

She ended the call and went back to her research. Maybe she should change her tactics and search small newspapers and see what they did instead of the big papers.

By the time she was due to leave for lunch, she'd gotten nowhere. The smaller newspapers were all doing the same types of stories as she was already doing, which wasn't enough.

Kendall slid her laptop and notebook into her bag before taking a moment to let down her curly blonde hair from the bun she'd shoved it into earlier. She didn't want to look a mess when she met with her dad even if her whole career was one.

The pub was a ten-minute walk from her office, so she left her car there and headed out on foot. She'd likely go home after lunch, but the walk would be good for counteracting all the fries she was about to eat.

Hoping the walk would also clear her head, she set out for the pub. Danny's always had good food, and if she couldn't get anything else right today, she could at least eat well.

"Kendall!" her dad yelled from across the pub when she entered.

She smiled and waved, used to his loud nature. He'd been the loudest her whole life. There was no point being embarrassed by it anymore, since everyone in here knew him by name and that he was loud.

"Hey, Dad," she said as she slid into the booth.

The pub was like a second home to her, and she smiled as she looked around. She waved at the people she knew as she took in the dark wood everywhere and all the sports photos and autographs on the wall.

It was an eclectic mix of all things sports. If there was a competition of any kind, they'd broadcast it here, bet on it, and get autographs from everyone involved, winners and losers both.

"I already put our order in." He slid her soda across to her. "What's going on with your job?"

She let her shoulders slump. "I can't do anything right. Nothing I write about is good enough."

"Your writing is damn good!" he defended her, ending his declaration with a thump on the table from his fist to drive his point home.

"The problem isn't my writing skills, it's my topics. They aren't 'hard-hitting' enough for my boss, and unless I can come up with something better by tomorrow, then I'm out." It hurt to even say it out loud.

"Nonsense. We're fighters, you and I. You'll come up with something," he assured her.

Rich, her dad, had been a fighter, not her. He believed that because he was one of the best boxers during his time that his talent passed on to her. It hadn't, sadly. She was in the corner here with no fancy moves to get out.

"I read your last article. It's good work," Grady, the owner, told her as he carried their food to the table.

"Thanks," she mumbled, not wanting to even explain why he'd probably never read another one.

"Thanks, Grady. I'll catch up with you in a few."

"You got it, Rich. Let me know if you need anything."

Her dad waited until Grady was out of earshot before he spoke again. "What if I could give you a story?"

"Like what?" she asked as she shoved fries into her mouth.

"First you have to promise not to be mad." The serious look on his face told her she was definitely going to be mad.

"Explain." She slid her plate away and listened.

"I've been coaching this fighter. He's really good."

"You're supposed to be retired! Taking it easy, considering moving to Florida." They'd been over this so many times. She knew he'd been up to something, but she didn't think he'd been coaching.

Instantly on the defense, he held his hands up. "I'm not in the ring," he assured her. "That's not even the part you won't like."

Kendall arched a brow at him and waited for him to continue. Why couldn't even lunch go right today?

"There's an underground MMA ring, and there's a fight tonight."

"How underground?" She'd write about it, but she didn't want to do anything that her dad would get in trouble for.

"It's not illegal—it's just not well known," he said cautiously.

"So, if I wrote about it, would anyone get in trouble?" She was a terrible reporter. This was exactly the type of thing she needed to do to keep her job.

"No. Some might be less than thrilled about the attention, but no one would get in trouble with the law." Using both hands, he picked up his burger. "Just come tonight, and then you can decide." Taking a massive bite from it, he smiled at her, clearly done talking about it.

"I'll think about it."

She pulled her plate back to her and picked up her own burger. Her dad sat there, grinning at her, knowing she'd come tonight even as she debated it. Hell, she knew she'd be there, even if there was no story.

She didn't know anything about MMA other than the fact that she'd watched a match or two with her father before. Watched was a loose definition. She'd played on her phone as he watched it, and she cheered when he did.

"Fine, but I don't know about the story part. I'll come and support you though," she told him and took a bite of her burger.

"That's all I ask," he replied, and his grin didn't fade a bit.

She'd have to go home and do some research before the match so she could at least look like she knew what she was doing there. Not that she had time for that.

Chapter Two

Chad sat in the locker room, doing his deep breathing to calm his mind before his fight tonight. This was only his second fight with Rich as his coach, but he felt better prepared than he ever had been before.

He'd already warmed up with Rich before, and now he was trying to harness all his energy for the fight. His muscles were warmed and ready, and his mind was getting there too.

A trainer sat across from him, wrapping his hands before he put his gloves on. The tape would provide a little more protection beneath the gloves for his knuckles, which were going to take a beating, or rather give one, if he remained focused.

Once his hands were taped, he was ready to walk out whenever they called him, but he still had a good half hour. Rich had taught him that being prepared early helped you stay focused, and so far, he agreed with the man.

He'd met Rich in the gym, and after only an hour with him, Chad had begged him to train him. Rich was older, and he was a boxer, not a mixed martial arts fighter, but the control Chad was learning from him was more valuable than anything other coaches had taught him.

Fighting Chance

Fighting had been the one thing he'd been doing his whole life with little success. He had always gotten good grades, but he couldn't take on the largest guy after school and win. He'd never dreamed of even making it this far, and if he did well here, he knew he had a shot at taking it to the real-deal fights, like UFC.

One day, he might make it that far. It had been his dream for longer than he could remember. It would also really stick it to all those people that said fighting wouldn't get him anywhere.

Growing up as a nerd, he was always bullied, and fighting had been something he wanted to learn. As an adult, his image had changed, thanks to the people he'd paid to help him with that transition, but this, fighting and winning, was the last thing that he needed to complete his image change.

He'd gotten tattoos, too, much to the concern of the image consultant, but they didn't show when he was wearing a suit and tie. He'd gotten those tattoos for himself as he'd bulked up from the training, needing to see himself differently in and out of clothes.

The image, the tattoos, the fighting, it all reflected his transition from the nerdy kid he'd been to the respected adult that women wanted and men wanted to be. No one would see the tattoos, except the women, but he knew they were there and how intimidating having them made him feel and look underneath his suit.

"How are you feeling?" Rich asked as he entered the locker room.

"I'm feeling good about this one," Chad told him, holding his taped hands out for inspection.

"Good, good." Rich checked over his tape and helped him slide his gloves on.

"Dad?" a woman's voice said from the locker room door.

"We're decent. You can come in," Rich answered.

A blonde woman walked in, wearing jeans and a plain T-shirt, her smile nearly knocking him out of his seat. She was beautiful, and now he was distracted. Shit.

"I just wanted to let you know I was here and wish you luck." She kissed Rich on the cheek.

"Chad, this is my daughter, Kendall. Kendall, meet Chad."

"So, you're the guy that got my dad to come out of retirement when he is supposed to be relaxing?" Her hands came to her hips, and he felt like a kid in school being scolded by the teacher.

"Calm it down. He needs a clear head. You can yell at him later," Rich told her.

Visions of her angry and yelling at him danced across his mind. Then came visions of making up after she was done being mad.

He shook his head. This was exactly what he didn't need. Not to mention that, as she was Rich's daughter, there was no one more off-limits than she was.

Now wasn't the time in his life for the complications that women brought. He knew better. He had a few women he could call for a good night, and he needed nothing beyond that—or so he told himself.

"Fine." She sent him a glare before turning her attention back on Rich. "There's a lot of people out there for something that isn't that well known." She arched a brow at Rich.

"Glad to see we have a good turnout. You going to be able to get a seat?"

She rolled her eyes. "I'm sure I can squeeze in somewhere."

"Well, you best get off and do that before there's nowhere left for you," Rich told her.

Kendall's jaw fell for just a second before she recovered. "Did you just dismiss me?" She pressed a hand to her chest in shock, her smile showing it was all a joke.

Rich shrugged. "Gotta get Chad ready for the fight."

"Fine. Guess I'll go make sure I can find a seat now."

"Sit up higher so you can see the whole fight," Rich advised as he hugged her.

"You act like I'm new at this," she laughed as she turned toward the door. "Good luck, Chad," she added to him before she left.

"I didn't know you had a daughter, Rich," Chad pointed out.

"I don't mix family with fighting often."

8

Which made Chad wonder why he was doing that now. Rich was a private man, always had been. Even at his peak as a boxer, he'd frustrated reports by remaining largely quiet on anything personal.

"Back to the breathing," Rich reminded him.

"Right." Chad sat up tall and tried to focus.

He pushed everything from his mind, including the fight, and focused on his breaths. Meditation wasn't something he ever would have bought into, but Rich had convinced him. The best part was it had worked.

Setting his mind free of all his worries right before any fight, even a practice one, had helped him immensely. He went into fights focused, ready, and won more often than not.

His punches had improved, as had his accuracy since starting with Rich. Next week he had a training session with someone Rich knew to work on his takedowns, something that Rich wasn't as able to help him with.

Chad knew he'd come a long way in just a few months. He listened to everything Rich told him, which was different than he'd done with any other coach,

"Focus," Rich reminded him, knowing his thoughts were wandering.

He pushed the thoughts away for later and went back to focusing on his breath. In through the nose and out through the mouth.

Someone knocked on the door and said, "They're ready for you."

"Tell them we're coming," Rich called back before looking at Chad. "Remember, tonight isn't about winning, it's about your skill level. Get out there and focus on what you're doing."

It was the same advice he'd given before the last fight. Chad nodded. He was still working on that focus, but damned if he wasn't trying.

Chad stood up and let Rich lead him out of the locker room and down the hall to the octagon. Kendall hadn't been exaggerating. The place was packed—more so than he'd ever seen it.

"Don't look at anyone. Just keep your mind on your breathing and your goal," Rich reminded him.

He was grateful for the reminder because he found he wanted to look for Kendall but kept his gaze neutral instead. He didn't make eye contact with anyone as he entered the ring and waved his arms to pump up the crowd.

The crowd played into his request and got louder from every angle. His opponent was already in the octagon, which meant the fight was soon to start.

The cage was closed, leaving just him, the other man he'd be fighting, and the ref inside. He took stock of his opponent. The man was from out of town, and although Chad had watched a few recordings of his fights, it was different seeing a man in person.

He seemed evenly matched to him in size. Chad's fighting skills were better, based on what he'd seen in the videos, though. He hoped they were. Three rounds were exhausting for both fighters, but if one had the upper hand from the start, it used considerably less energy.

"Men, touch gloves and wait for my signal."

Chad moved forward, his glove quickly making contact with the other fighter's before he backed away. The referee stood between them with his arm up.

His arm came down, cutting the tension between them like a knife. "Fight!"

Chapter Three

The one thing you couldn't miss in the stands was the intensity of the crowd. They cheered and jeered during each fight.

"Come here often?" asked the man next to her.

She turned her head to face him. He was an older man, probably late fifties with a gap in his smile, but seemed nice overall. "First time," she told him.

"Not a lot of women like this sort of thing."

They were between fights. Chad's being the headline fight, it was the next and final fight of the night.

"I'm not most women," she joked. "My dad is Rich Williams."

The man's eyes lit up with recognition. "Well, ain't that just something?"

"Indeed." She didn't hide who her father was, though that was probably what had landed her a sports reporter job that she was no good at.

"I heard he's coaching the fella in the next fight?" the man asked.

She nodded and stuck out her hand. "I'm Kendall."

He shook it. "Name's Lewy."

"Nice to meet you, Lewy."

The first fighter came out into the ring, and the crowd jeered. Clearly, he was not a fan favorite. One thing she did know was that it didn't matter how good or bad the home team was—they were always the favorite, no matter the sport.

Chad entered the ring next, and she took the time to really study him. She'd met him briefly but hadn't had the chance to look him over without being obvious about it.

His muscular body was on display now and she took her time appraising him as he walked around. She knew he'd be fit—you had to be to do this, and her father wouldn't be helping him if he wasn't in top physical form—but damn, he was hot.

Tattoos crawled up his right arm and across his chest, his left arm bare. She wanted to inspect them, know what they were and why he'd gotten them. She licked her lips at the thought.

She'd thought herself immune, having grown up around sweaty, shirtless fighters. Apparently, she'd been very wrong because her thoughts were drifting in a very unprofessional direction.

With every circle he made around the ring, raising his arms to gear up the crowd, she could see the muscles of his back and chest flex and pull with each movement. It was mesmerizing.

Her dad stood off to the side of the ring but outside it. The only three people within the octagon were the two fighters and the one referee.

She watched as Chad remained calm, observing his opponent from the center of the cage as he bounced from foot to foot in a circle around him. That was good, she thought. Let the other guy wear himself out.

Chad bluffed a strike a few times, just barely jutting at the other man before going back to his stance. The other man had backed away from them but was now increasing his footwork, and she knew he'd strike soon.

No sooner than she'd thought it, the other man jabbed one arm out, connecting only with Chad's glove. Clearly, he had been watching and waiting too. The other man tried again but made no connection.

The crowd was urging Chad to strike, but he remained patient, seeming as though he couldn't hear anyone yelling.

"Your dad has trained him well, getting him working on patience and focus."

Kendall smiled. That was exactly how her father did things.

"I've seen Chad go a few rounds, boxing with other people in the gym. He's impressive and explosive when he decides to move."

She believed Lewy. Chad looked like he was holding back.

In the blink of an eye, Chad exploded and landed hit after hit on his opponent. The other man was quickly taken to the ground as Chad wrapped him up, still throwing punches.

His opponent managed to get free, but he seemed winded already from the effort he put into just the first round. The man was pissed, that much was obvious.

The ref signaled the end of the round, and it was clear to Kendall that Chad had taken this one. He didn't seem to be out of breath either, whereas the other man was ranting at his coach, his breathing rapid.

Round two went about the same way. If there were more rounds in this fight, the man would easily just wear himself out. Lewy yelled next to her, matching the chorus of the rest of the crowd chanting at Chad to take the man down.

The third round was short. Chad was on him in the first few seconds, taking him to the ground, landing blow after blow before pinning him down. It felt like forever but could only have been a few seconds before the man finally tapped out.

Much like in boxing, the referee took Chad's arm and raised it in the air as he declared him the winner. She had no idea what was said after that as the crowd exploded with energy.

She watched as Chad left the octagon and headed out of the crowded area. Fortunately, she'd found her story, but could she maintain a safe distance from it?

The crowd dwindled as she sat there, waiting before going back to find her dad. She thought about how her dad had been married and divorced five times, the first of them with Kendall's mother, who'd left her with Rich when she split.

She reminded herself of that fact over and over as she made her way to the locker room. There was no room in her life for a fighter. If her thoughts kept going in that direction, though, she might make room in her bed for Chad and get him out of her system.

If he had what it took to make it in this world, it was going to require all of his time, no breaks. She'd watched her father rise up through the boxing world and imagined it was the same for MMA.

Shaking her head, she laughed at herself. She'd barely met the man and was over here talking herself out of a future with him like they were something. She was a fool.

Knocking on the locker room door like she'd done a million times before felt strange when Chad called out an answer instead. Carefully, she opened the door, looking around in case she needed to back out quickly.

"Rich went to find the trainer." Chad lifted his still-gloved hands to show her why he left.

She let herself walk all the way in. "Dad didn't just do it?"

Chad shook his head. "His arthritis doesn't let him grip hard enough all the time. He helped me put them on, and that took more effort than he liked."

She was a fool for doing it, but she sat on the bench across from him. "I can help if you want. I've done it for Dad plenty of times."

"If you don't mind, I wouldn't say no. I'm ready to get them off," he answered, attempting to flex his fingers.

"You can't get these off on your own?" she asked, looking at his exposed fingers as she inspected the glove.

"I can, usually, but I got some good blows in, and I think I'm a little swollen."

The gloves were unstrapped, and she could tell he'd pulled at the left one already. She slid her fingers under the bottom of the glove and gave it a good yank, budging a little.

"Okay, it's really on there. I'm going to pull, and when I do, you pull too," she instructed him, putting her feet against his bench as she got ready to give it a pull.

"Thanks," he said, blowing out a breath as his left hand popped free.

They repeated the same process, freeing his right hand too. She moved without thinking and instantly started unwrapping the white tape around his knuckles.

He'd said they were a bit swollen, and she'd have to agree. Kendall moved as she had a thousand times before and brought the bucket of ice water over for him to put his hands in.

"Thanks," Chad told her as he hissed, sliding his hands into it.

"No problem."

She looked around at the locker room that could use a coat of paint. A dull gray color flaked away in many places, revealing a blue underneath. The benches were the same ones she'd seen in here as a child, the wood having lost most of its lacquer years ago.

"Found him," Dad said as he swung the door open.

The trainer slid in behind him, looking terrified. Clearly, her dad had laid into him before returning with him.

"Oh, you've already got your hands soaking. Good." He looked at Kendall. "You helped?"

"I did," she confirmed.

"Well, get them out. Let the trainer have a look before he disappears again," he told Chad.

The trainer, a young man, probably about her age, came around quickly to look at his hands. They spoke for a moment as she watched, and then the trainer poked at Chad's ribs before finally leaving.

"That dude's an idiot," Rich said.

"Come on, Dad, everything is fine," Kendall said, trying to keep him from going on a rant.

"No, it's not. You get paid for a job, then you should be doing that job. It's ridiculous that I had to go chase him down and get him in here when he should already be here, waiting."

The tirade she'd seen coming was now underway. She cut her eyes to Chad who was looking up at her dad, smiling. This wasn't new for him, then.

His rant tapered off when he caught them both smiling at him. "Knock it off. You're both crazy." He waved his hands at them. "What did you think, kiddo?"

"It was intense for sure. I had no idea this was going on."

"So maybe we'll be seeing you around more often?"

"Maybe," she answered. It all depended on what her boss thought of the story.

Chapter Four

Kendall had stayed up all night writing a story about the fight. She'd done all the digging, and while they treated the event like it was underground, it actually had all the permits.

It might grow more popular because she wrote about it, if her story was chosen. She wrote about it from the angle of being underground to keep it edgy. Hopefully that's what Robert was looking for. If this didn't win him over, she was throwing in the towel and switching careers entirely. She just wasn't cut out for it.

She was exhausted but had been up since before her alarm went off despite having had only three hours of sleep. Checking her hair in the mirror, she fixed her flyaways and headed out.

Stopping for coffee was never in her schedule in the morning, mostly because she was always running late. If she got the go ahead to write this article, she wouldn't need to come in so early anymore either because she would technically be working nights. She would only have to come in on Monday mornings for the staff meetings.

The thought that she might get to write about the fight made her smile. She was feeling more confident about today than she had ever before in this job.

The smile held until she walked into the building. All the confidence she'd had was replaced with nerves.

"Morning," Sindee greeted her as she came in.

Kendall groaned. She wasn't in the mood for pleasantries right now.

"How did the story go last night? Did you write it?"

"I did." She sighed. "I don't know if it's enough."

"Kendall!" Robert yelled across the floor.

"I'm sure it's great!"

Sindee's chipper attitude was too much to deal with right now. Kendall grabbed her laptop and headed to Robert's office.

"What did you come up with?" He walked around his desk and practically fell into his chair.

He was a portly man. Round was the only way to describe him, and when he yelled, which was all the time, he looked like an overripe tomato.

"I have an article about MMA fighting, here, locally."

She pulled out her laptop and brought the article up before passing him the whole thing. Sitting didn't seem like the right thing to do when your career was on the line, so she stood, fidgeting as little as possible.

He looked it over and made a few grunts but didn't say anything else. She gripped her hands together behind her back until they hurt just to keep from moving too much and distracting him. Any distraction might piss him off and have him saying no to all of it.

"How'd you find out about this?" he asked.

"A source," she replied.

"I'll bet." He passed the laptop back. "It'll work for now. Get it over to the editors and have another one ready for Saturday. After that, I want twice weekly stories. Break the article up some. Give them just enough to complete the article, and then move the rest to the next day. Got it?"

"Y-yes, sir."

"Good. We'll see if you do or not."

Dismissed, she backed up, hitting her lower back on the door handle. She spun, pulled it open, and headed for her desk.

"I can't tell—how'd it go?" Sindee asked.

"I— umm. He liked it," Kendall said and sat at her desk in shock.

"Yay! That's good news, so act like it!"

"You're right. I'm just still shocked."

"I don't know why you always are. Just take the happy things that come to you. You know you're a talented journalist."

Kendall smiled back at her. "Thanks."

"I have to go, but you've got this!"

Sindee swept away, and Kendall set her laptop up. She needed to get the article submitted and then figure out what to write about next and how to drag the series out.

She'd agreed to meet her father for lunch today, so she set about getting everything she could done before then. She needed to find out when the next fight was and how to get interviews.

It didn't take long to spruce up the article and submit it. She'd have some edits to do after lunch, but it was turned in.

Kendall spent the rest of her time mapping out a goal of articles to write. She knew not everyone would want to talk to her, but she wanted to give it her best shot, so she made it into a wish list, containing everything she'd want in a perfect world to complete the series of articles.

If it all worked out as planned, she could milk this for at least two months with one article running in every paper on Wednesdays and Saturdays. That was at least a benefit to working for a small paper—she didn't have to do it daily.

After packing up, she let her curls out of the loose knot she'd had them in and then headed out.

"Where are you going?" John, another journalist, asked.

"Lunch," she answered.

He annoyed her and hated that she was doing sports. His grin was always plastered on his face whenever Robert didn't like her articles.

"Oh, so you're not fired?" he asked.

She shook her head, making her curls bounce, before answering, "Nope, afraid not. You're still stuck with me." She added a pout at the end just to make herself a little more feminine because it would irritate him.

"You might be able to pull off this article, but I doubt it will keep you going for long, and you'll be out of here in no time."

"Speaking of time—" She looked down at her non-existent watch on her wrist. "—I've gotta go to lunch now. Bye."

He absolutely grated on her nerves. No matter how good or bad she was doing, he was always there to kick her. Walking away from him while she was on a high note, though—that made her feel good.

She hurried to the pub, anxious to tell her dad what had happened. The smile she'd worn earlier was back in place despite John attempting to kick her while she was down.

Dad arrived at the same time as she did. "Hey, kiddo," he greeted her.

"Hey, Dad."

They walked in together and went back to the same booth they'd always sat in. Grady quickly came around with their drinks and confirmed they were getting their usual orders.

"Thanks." She smiled at Grady as he walked away.

"How did it go?" Dad took a sip of his beer.

"It went great! Not only did he like my article, but he wants one for each paper going forward."

"That's great, kiddo. I knew you could do it." He beamed at her.

"Thank you for the idea. It was just what I needed."

"So, this means I'm off the hook for not telling you about the coaching, right?"

She'd scold him later for it, and for the beer he was having with lunch when he was supposed to be eating healthier. For now, she was just happy to not be looking for a new job, thanks to his help.

"You're off the hook for now," she assured him.

"I'll take what I can get."

"I do need something though." She pulled out her notebook.

"I'll tell you what I can. I don't want my name on it though."

She knew that, and had no intention of writing an article on him. "I have questions, but not to quote you. You're my confidential source." She gave him a wink.

"Well then, what do you need?"

She led with what she thought would be the easiest thing to get. "I want to interview Chad."

"I'm not saying no, but I don't know that he will go for it," he cautioned.

Damn, that had been what she thought would be easiest. "Why not?"

"His story is his to tell. It's not my place."

At that cryptic final statement, she put her notebook away. Apparently, she'd gotten all she could for now.

Their food arrived shortly after, so she let the subject change and just chatted over lunch. She was going to regret the second greasy burger with a giant plate of fries, but regrets were for later—for now, she'd enjoy it. Besides, both burgers had different reasons: one was pity and one was happiness.

They finished up, and she got his training schedule and permission to show up. Well, she got a warning not to "distract his fighter", but he didn't say she couldn't come. She'd just try to talk to Chad after.

Laying low was her plan. She might even get in her own workout after all these carbs. She'd just go work out at the gym and chat with him after they were done. It was a solid plan.

Smile still permanently in place, she paid for lunch after arguing with her dad about it and set off to get ready for the gym. On the bright side, everything she was involved in happened later in the day, so for the next while, she was free to be her night owl self and sleep as late as she wanted.

Toni Denise

It was going to be a great day—she just knew it. It had started out so well that there was no way anything could bring her down now.

Chapter Five

Kendall was running behind, as usual, and didn't get to the gym until practice was well underway. It had been so long since she'd been to the gym to visit her father that a weird sort of nostalgia settled over her as she looked around.

This gym, while very popular with the locals, had seen better days, but oddly, it looked the same as she remembered it. The hanging punching bags were well-worn with faded paint from overuse. The number of pictures on the wall had grown, but she recognized right away the ones of her father that had been there longer than she could remember.

A glass case was on the wall near a desk. The only thing that served any sort of modern-era gym technology expectations was the computer on that old desk. She smiled as she walked over to greet Tommy, who was sitting behind it.

"Hi, Tommy," she said as she approached.

"Well, hi there, Ms. Kendall. Haven't seen you in an age." He stood up and came around the desk to give her a hug.

"I'm just here to watch Dad's new protégé. Is it all right if I sneak on over?" She knew it would be. They'd never charge her even if she was coming to work out, but she felt it was only right to ask.

"Of course! Make sure you don't sneak out without a proper goodbye, now," he teased and went back around the desk.

She walked over to where some chairs were lined up and she could see the boxing ring. It seemed that today Chad was only boxing, which was something she hadn't expected from him.

Her dad looked up and gave her a small smile before going back to yelling at Chad in the ring. It was the only acknowledgment she'd get from him until the match was over. She knew how it worked and wasn't bothered by it.

"Kendall!" a man's voice called to her.

She turned to see a few people she recognized from her father's fighting days approaching her. Staying seated, she just waved back, hoping to get back to watching the match soon.

"Tommy told us you were here, so we just wanted to come see how you were," Mack told her.

"Hi, Mack. Just came to watch Dad's hard work. Making sure he's not overdoing it, you know?"

"Now, Kendall, you know we wouldn't let him in that ring."

Just then, as Mack tried to tell her that her father wasn't over-doing things, he yelled and slammed a folding chair down against the hard floor, drawing everyone's attention.

Mack put up both his hands in surrender. "I only said he wasn't in the ring."

"Yeah...," she trailed off.

She wasn't really here to watch her father, but she knew these men and they'd have something to say if she told them she was here to watch Chad instead. Everyone in this gym had told her at least once she shouldn't date a fighter. That wasn't her plan, but they'd make it known how they felt about it, and it would become a thing, and she didn't want to go there if she could avoid it.

"He's got talent," Mack remarked as he took a seat next to her.

She looked back at the ring and couldn't help but agree as she watched him. "Dad is teaching him well."

"There's a lot of your dad in him for sure, but you can only use what Rich is telling him to do if you have the raw talent. You should see him in the octagon." Mack watched the fight as he spoke.

"I have, just the other night. He's impressive, for sure." A thought came to her mind. "How did Dad end up coaching him? He's not MMA."

"Persistence." Mack threw his head back in laughter. "Damnedest thing. Chad showed up one day out of the blue, looking for Rich. Rich wouldn't even talk to the kid. So, he showed up over and over again every day and worked out near Rich, but he only tried once each day to talk to him. After a week or so, Rich finally agreed to hear him out just to get him to stop following him around. I don't know what they talked about exactly, but after that, Rich started training him." Mac ended his story with a shrug.

"Wow. Dad didn't tell me any of that."

"Your dad understands more than most about keeping his life private, so I assume the kid swore him to confidence. That's something that Rich wouldn't break for anyone."

Kendall nodded. He wouldn't break anyone's trust or spill a secret. He was the least gossipy person she knew. Her mother must have been a real gossip for Kendall to have turned out half as nosy as she did and then to become a journalist on top of that.

Silently, she went back to watching the match, or maybe just watching Chad. His patience was something that she'd seen in few fighters, and she knew it was hard work to get there. He didn't spend any energy if he didn't need to, and at the end of the round, he would explode on the other man, getting solid hits in.

"He will take this match," Mack said. "I don't know why he insists on doing MMA. He's a skilled boxer and could go far in it."

Kendall added that question to her own growing list of ones she had about Chad. She just had to convince him to answer them.

The bell dinged, signaling the end of the round and the match.

Mack was right—Chad had taken it. The other fighter was bloody and pissed off, making it known that he disagreed by yelling angrily at anyone in his path.

"Out of my fucking way," the other man yelled as he pushed past the people in the crowd.

It was just a spar, so it wasn't like there were a lot of people to watch the match, just those who were already at the gym, judging by the gym shorts and tanks everyone was wearing.

"Kendall," her dad called.

"Thanks for keeping me company, Mack." She gave him a friendly smile before making her way around the ring to her dad.

"Hey, kiddo. Stay over here for now?" he requested.

She knew what that meant. It meant he was worried about how people were going to react, and he wanted her safe. The fighter seemed agitated, but she didn't notice anyone else who might cause a scene. Then again, she hadn't been paying much attention to anyone other than Chad.

Chad stood beside her now, looking down at her.

"Nice fight," she told him.

"Thanks," he said, his voice deep and more polished than she expected.

A moment later, he pushed her behind him as the other fighter came out of the locker room, still yelling. He kept a hand on her arm like he was making sure she stayed there.

"Keep an eye on her. I'll be right back," her dad told Chad without a glance in her direction.

Chad nodded and backed up into her. "If he comes this way, I need you to go to the exit, understand?"

She was torn. He was right, but at the same time she didn't want to seem the damsel in distress. Finally, she decided that appearances didn't matter and just agreed.

They both watched, her head peeking around him, as her father and a few other men yelled at the fighter and a handful of people who were with him. Things were getting more heated as the fighter lunged at her dad.

"He'll be fine," Chad told her.

He must had felt her tense when the man lunged. She took her eyes off the scene in front of her and looked around at the exits, planning how to leave if she needed to.

"Step back." Chad pressed into her with his back. "McDonnell is pissed and keeps looking over here."

Mack walked up from behind them, causing her to jump as his hand landed on her shoulder.

"Stay over here," Mack told Chad.

"I will as long as no fighting breaks out."

"I know you want to go over there, but the last thing you want to do is enrage him any further. Keep an eye on our Kendall here. I'm going to go stand with Rich," Mack told him as he walked away.

"I should just go," she told Chad. Not that she didn't need to interview him, but she didn't want to be in here when all hell broke loose.

Chad gripped her arm. "No."

"You can't tell me no." She jerked her arm out of his hand.

"McDonnell has seen you over here with me this whole time. I can tell you that he's a violent idiot, and if you leave, you risk him attacking you because he's pissed off at me." He never turned to face her, keeping his eyes on the commotion.

She let out a small sigh and went back to watching the chaos. When put like that, he was right, and she wasn't going to argue with him.

"It's about to get bad." She could feel the tension of the whole gym going on high alert.

"Yep." Chad dropped his hands from her as he turned to face her. "You've been in this gym a few times before, right?"

She nodded as she split her gaze between him and the fighter.

"Listen to me. When he makes a break for it, which is going to be really soon, I want you to go under the ring and wait until you have a clear shot for the ladies' locker room. When you get there, lock yourself in."

Her eyes widened as she looked up at him. "Okay."

"Is he still looking this way?" Chad asked, his back to the fighter.

She glanced back at them and accidentally connected her gaze with McDonnell's. "Shit. He's looking right at me."

"New plan, I'm going to walk you to your car and see if he stays here. Where did you park?" he asked.

"Around back like everyone else."

"Great. Get your keys out."

Her hands were shaking, but she managed to pull them out of her small purse. Chad took them from her and then opened her hand, weaving them into her grip with one key sticking out between each finger.

"Hold them like that. I assume you know how to throw a punch from your dad, but if you have to use it, this will stun him enough to get away." He spun her around. "Keep me between you and them at all times. We're going to move quick, but try to look casual. Got it?"

Her heart was racing as they moved. The yelling was getting louder, and she tried to turn to see what was going on.

"Don't." Chad stopped her. "You need to get out of here. I don't know why Rich thought it would be a good idea for you to come tonight anyway."

"Don't blame him."

"Let's argue later."

Finally reaching the back door, Kendall pushed it open and stepped outside.

"Keep going," Chad pressed. "Which car?"

"Th-that one," she pointed.

They were nearly there when the back door crashed open, and McDonnell charged them.

"Go" was all Chad said and Kendall sprinted the last few feet to her car, barely getting inside before McDonnell's fist connected with Chad's jaw.

Chapter Six

He was used to fighting, but it'd admittedly been a while since he got into one outside any rings. His face fucking hurt like hell and his rib was likely bruised, but he managed to pin the other man to the ground long enough for the police to show up.

The second they did, he stood and put his hands up, knowing full well what it was going to look like. Sure enough, they yelled at him, guns drawn, to put his hands on the car.

Unfortunately, it was Kendall's car, which meant she was now watching this humiliation. He felt her eyes on him as he looked down at her trunk.

Her presence tonight had been unexpected, but he'd known she was there the moment she walked in. He felt her long before he saw her, and it had damn near cost him the round.

Then she'd taken a seat and started to watch the fight and it was all he could do to keep from looking over at her. Stupidly, he'd thought he might get a chance to talk to her after the fight but then McDonnell had lost his shit.

That was the problem with winning—someone always had to

lose, and they usually weren't very happy about it when they did. Thankfully, it didn't escalate to this level often, but if anyone was going to take it too far, it would have been this guy.

The car door opened as the cops approached, and Kendall stood up out of her vehicle.

She immediately put herself between him and the cops. "Officers, that man chased us out of the gym."

It was different, having someone come to his defense. He wasn't sure how to feel about it other than to be pissed that she was potentially putting herself in danger.

"We need you to step away," he heard someone tell her.

"Why?" she asked.

"All we know is, when we got here, that man had the other one on the ground. Now we need to talk to everyone involved."

"I was involved too. I saw it all." She backed up a bit closer to him, and he could feel the heat coming off her body.

"It's okay, Kendall—they're just doing their job," he told her, praying she would step away.

"No. There's no reason for you to be treated like you did something wrong," she explained.

Now that the fear had passed, her anger was seeping back in. He appreciated that it wasn't directed at him, but she would still be in danger if she didn't let the police do their jobs.

"Sir, would you please stand?" an officer asked him.

He did, and stepped to Kendall's side so she was no longer in front of him. Two officers came up then, and one sat a clipboard on her trunk as the other looked them over.

"Some girlfriend you have here. I think she would have gone to jail for you if you were in the wrong here," the shorter officer said.

"She's not my girlfriend," Chad told them.

"Well, might want to fix that," the taller quipped and laughed at his own joke.

The next hour was spent answering questions and then answering the same ones again. He'd been questioned before. Hell, he'd been arrested more than once, so he knew how this was going to go. Kendall was getting angrier with each question.

"This is enough," she told the short officer. "He needs medical attention, and we've already answered everything twice. You have all our contact information, so you can reach out if there's anything else."

Her hands were on her hips, and there was fire in her eyes. He reached out and put a hand on her shoulder, trying to bring her some peace, but she shrugged him off.

"I'm tired, cranky, hungry, and I'm over this. We did nothing wrong here, and they are treating us like we did."

"We really need you to calm down. It's important to have all the information."

Kendall tilted her head as she looked at the shorter officer. He'd given his name at some point, but Chad had forgotten, or hadn't cared enough to listen.

"You know I can see that you have already arrested the other guy, right? Which means that between our story and everyone else inside, you already have all the information."

"Kendall," Chad warned.

She was taking it too far to be out here arguing with the police. He didn't know where Rich was, but he was positive if Kendall got arrested, he'd no longer have a coach even if she'd done it to herself.

"I think we do have all we need, but you can't go back inside for now. We are still questioning folks, and for now, it's a crime scene."

Chad nodded, having assumed this would happen. "Can I have an escort to get my keys?" he asked.

Tall officer shook his head. "Nothing and no one in or out right now."

"Thanks," he muttered. So now he was stuck out here with no shirt and nowhere to go.

"Sorry, that's out of our hands," the short one said and shrugged as they walked away.

"Come on," Kendall said, unlocking her car.

He whipped his head around to face her. "What?"

"You can come back to my place. I'm sure Dad will grab your stuff when he gets sprung out of there, and he can bring it by. I'll just text him and let him know where you're at," she said as if it was that simple.

"Your dad—"

She cut him off. "Can't leave. You can but can't go anywhere, so just come on before they decide to ask us everything for a third time."

Resigned, he walked to the passenger side and got in. He knew this was probably a bad idea, but he didn't want to stay here.

The ride to her place was only about fifteen minutes, and neither of them said a word on the way. Oddly, it wasn't awkward. It was a comfortable silence, and she didn't attempt to ask him about the fight or anything the officers had asked him about his past.

"Come on," she said as she opened the lobby door to her apartment building.

Chad followed despite every alarm in his head going off and telling him not to go inside with her. Rich was going to kick his ass, he knew it, but he followed her in anyway.

She held the door for him when they reached her apartment and then shut and locked it behind him. "Dad has a key," she explained. "No need to invite trouble by leaving it unlocked."

He nodded and took in her cozy living room. It suited her. Gray with pops of a cheerful yellow decorated the furniture and the curtains.

"Dad's got some stuff here from when he and Cheryl broke up. I think we should at least be able to get you cleaned up."

She went down the hallway and turned into one of the rooms. He stopped short of following her and waited outside the bathroom door for her to come back.

Kendall handed him a stack of clothes and then opened another door before handing him a towel and washcloth. "I'm afraid I only have my soap in there, but you're welcome to use it. I'm going to go collapse on the couch."

He only nodded as she walked away. Chad closed the bathroom

door, and then he took a minute to look into the mirror and instantly regretted it. He knew it would be bad. He made it a point not to look at himself immediately after a fight.

He turned the water on, then he looked through the clothes she had brought him. Just a pair of gym shorts and a plain T-shirt. Hopefully, Rich wouldn't be too mad about it.

After quickly showering, he got dressed and found Kendall right where she said she would be on the couch. Taking a seat next to her, he hissed until he was able to straighten out again. The pain in his ribs would be a bit much for the next few days until he got used to it again.

"I knew you were hurt." Kendall stood up and walked away before he could protest.

She returned a minute later with a first aid kit and a bag. She rummaged in the bag for a minute before pulling out a long bandage.

"Stand up," she told him.

"You don't have to do that. I'm fine."

She leveled him with a look, and he stopped arguing and stood up.

"Thank you."

He watched as she reached back into the bag and pulled out a tub of some kind of cream. Taking a scoop of it, she rubbed it between her hands before putting them on him.

It was pure torture. Not the pain, but to have her hands on him when all he could do was think about math in an effort to keep his dick from getting hard.

Not quickly enough, she wrapped his ribs before telling him to sit again. Both sad and happy that it was over, he took a seat as she took his hand to inspect it.

"This all from the parking lot?" she asked.

He tried for a joke. "Yeah, I should have left my gloves on, apparently."

"You probably wouldn't have been able to take him down quite so well if you had them on." She reached into the first aid kit, pulled out something else, and rubbed it over his busted knuckles one hand at a time.

He wondered what he'd done in his life to deserve this special kind of torture. When she finished, she stood up and packed everything away before taking it back out of the room.

"What was that cream?" he asked when she came back.

"It's something my dad used for bruises and sore muscles. It will help you relax some." She took a seat on one end of the couch and went back to watching the TV.

"You can go shower if you want to. I left my stuff in a pile in there, but I can grab it so if your dad shows up while you're in there, I can get out of your way."

"Don't leave while I'm gone, but I am going to go shower. What a freaking night."

He sat down on the couch, not paying any attention to the TV as he waited for her to come back. His phone had yet to go off with a call from Rich, and he didn't understand what was taking so long back at the gym.

Kendall came into the living room with her hair still damp. "Anything from Dad?" she asked.

"Nothing."

"What is going on there?"

"I genuinely don't know."

He tried to keep his eyes off her long legs that he could see so much more of now that she had put on such short shorts. They were dark blue with white trim and made his mind wander to places it definitely didn't need to go.

"Guess we might as well get comfortable," she told him.

"I'm good. Thanks for letting me come over." He meant it. He didn't know what he would've done other than sit in the parking lot if she hadn't made him come with her.

"Oh shoot, did you want something to drink or eat?" She jumped up.

"No, I'm good. Sit back down."

"You sure?"

"I'm fine, really."

"Okay." She sat down again and checked her phone. "Do you think something's wrong?" she asked.

"He knows you're fine. If he didn't, I don't think they'd be able to keep him there."

She thought about it and then set her phone back down again. He concentrated on not looking at her and did his best to focus on the TV.

As the movie rolled credits, he looked over to find her curled up asleep. He pulled a blanket off the back of the couch and carefully dropped it around her before sneaking into her kitchen and calling Rich.

He tried four times but got no answer. Something was wrong if he couldn't get through and Rich hadn't reached out to his daughter.

He called the gym and no one picked up. Unfortunately, those were the only numbers he had until Kendall woke up and he could ask her if there was anyone else they could call.

When he went back into the living room, Kendall had stretched out on the couch, leaving him nowhere to sit without touching her. That wasn't something he could do and keep himself in check, so he grabbed a pillow off the couch and stretched out on the floor after flipping the TV off. It was going to be a long night and an even longer day tomorrow if they didn't hear from Rich soon.

Chapter Seven

Confused, Kendall rubbed her eyes as she came awake. Light was coming through her living room's sheer curtains, and she was on the couch. It took her a moment, but when she remembered why she was on the couch, she jumped up only to step on Chad, making her fall.

"Oof," he said as she collapsed on top of him.

"I'm sorry." She scrambled away. "I didn't know you were there."

"You fell asleep, and I didn't get in touch with anyone, so I crashed for a little bit."

He sounded like he'd been awake for a lot longer than she had. He looked exhausted, if she was being honest, but still hot. She shook her head, clearing that thought. That was not what she needed to be thinking about.

"You never heard from anyone?" she asked.

He shook his head. "Nope. I called Rich and the gym and never got anyone."

"What the hell is going on?" She stood up and walked around Chad to get her phone. "No missed calls or messages for me either."

"I don't know," he said as he sat up.

"I'm so sorry you slept on the floor. You should have woken me up."

He shrugged. "I've slept on worse, and I didn't get much sleep anyway."

She didn't bother arguing, since it didn't matter. Right now, she just needed to find out where her dad was. "I'm going to try calling."

Chad nodded and lifted himself up to sit on the couch instead of the floor. He watched and waited for her to finally end the call with no answer.

She pulled up the number to the gym and called there too. Still no answer. It was early but she thought they'd be open.

"I'm going to get dressed, and then we can head down there," she told Chad as she walked away.

If he replied, she didn't hear him. She quickly threw on clothes that looked reasonably professional and fixed her hair before stopping to brush her teeth.

Chad was in the living room on his phone when she went back in. He held up a hand and then waved her over.

"I'm going to put you on speaker." He pulled the phone away from his ear and pushed a button. "Okay, Joe, I have Kendall here listening too."

"Well, it's a good thing you guys made it outside because all hell broke loose last night. In the end, everyone was arrested, and two of the guys with McDonnell were taken to the hospital. They're making everyone sit until the judge can see them, and that's looking like it might not be until this afternoon. I'm going to head down there. I'll call you back if I hear anything more."

"Thanks, man. Is anyone at the gym?"

"Nope. It's pretty rough in there from last night, and I think everyone with a key to open the door is locked up right now."

"Shit. Thanks."

Chad hung up the phone and looked over at Kendall. She was

white as a ghost, and he was pretty sure he could have knocked her over with a feather.

"Sit down." He gave her hand a small pull and she dropped onto the couch. "It's going to be fine. There's camera in the gym, so it will all get sorted out." He hoped it would, anyway.

"You seem rather calm considering everything going on."

"It's not that I'm not worried. We just can't do anything at the moment. Hell, I can't even get my keys to go home at this point or my car," he reminded her.

Deflated, Kendall sat back on the couch. He was right. As much as she wanted to head down there, it wouldn't do any good at all except to piss her dad off.

"Is it cool if I stay here until I can get back into the gym? If not, I can call Joe back and see if he can come give me a ride."

"You can stay here. It's no problem. This just sucks. How'd he know what was going on anyway?"

"Joe's a cop."

Well, at least she knew the information was accurate, then. Even if it was crappy. Why would they arrest everyone?

"You can have the remote." Kendall stood up and headed for the kitchen. "I'm just going to get some work done, since I'm up anyway. Make yourself at home. There's food in the fridge."

She grabbed a yogurt and opened her laptop as she sat at the table. If nothing else, she'd get a head start on her next article. It wasn't going to be directly about Chad this time though. It was going to be about the fight, and why not?

Hours passed as she wrote two full length articles about the fight last night. Both fights—Chad's and then the one after. If her boss saw it her way, this was going to be a good thing. She'd left out the names, which was going to help tease her exclusive with him.

Odds were that only one of these stories would run, but she'd take the chance and submit both. If they didn't like either, then she'd pitch her series to Chad right away, but now just didn't feel like the right time.

She ran the articles through her editing software once more, doing her best to submit a polished piece of work for each one, hoping to impress.

"Hey." Chad stood in the kitchen, looking at her fridge. "Mind if I order something?" he asked.

She had to admit, her diet wasn't meant for someone training, and the definition of diet in her case was whatever was left from the last time she went grocery shopping two weeks ago—so not much.

"Go for it," she told him before adding, "From where?"

They talked over a few places before settling on one that Chad liked, and he put in an order for both of them. At least when it came to technology, he still had what he needed. She wasn't sure how he'd wound up with his phone, but shrugged it off.

"How'd you end up fighting?" Kendall asked while they waited for the food.

Chad let out a sigh, and she thought for sure he'd blow off her question.

"I was a geeky kid, always picked on. Even as an adult, people overlook the ones that they don't respect, and brains aren't always what helps your succeed. Often it's about appearances."

She mulled on that for a minute. "Why fighting, though? Seems to me a personal trainer would be a much safer way to get fit or bulk up."

"It would. I always wanted to know how to fight though. One thing led to another, and I was set on this path."

They sat in mutual silence until the food arrived. Interestingly, despite her brain being busy trying to picture Chad as anything like he'd said he was, the silence was comfortable.

Chad answered her door, getting the food and carrying it to the kitchen. Kendall quickly followed him there and shut her laptop, getting it out of the way so they could eat.

"What was it like growing up with Rich as a father?" Chad asked.

"Chaotic," she answered. "It wasn't an easy life, and while I love my father, very much, it wasn't the easiest upbringing. I had a million dads with everyone at the gym jumping in on everything, so dating was hard, and extracurriculars were non-existent because there was no one to come get me."

"I'm sorry." Chad gave her a genuine smile.

"It's okay. It wasn't bad, it just wasn't easy. But then, it's what made me who I am today, and I have to stay thankful for that."

"That's definitely one way to think of it." He sounded thoughtful.

"I mean, same goes for you. If you'd had an easy childhood, then you wouldn't be on this path you are now. I'm sure there are other things that you wouldn't have accomplished if not for the things you had to overcome."

She tried to stay positive about most things when they were out of her control. Not that she didn't have her moments, like with Robert right now, but eventually she'd find her way to the positive outcome of him pushing her. Eventually, but not today.

"That's one way of looking at it, but it would have been a whole lot nicer not to come home beaten up as a kid."

"I'm sorry. No one helped or stepped in?" she asked.

"Not really. I had one teacher who would keep me later sometimes, and I think that was her way of helping me. My parents were of no help. My father was disappointed that I didn't fight back or win. My mother, well—she just did whatever my dad said."

He said it so casually, and Kendall's heart broke for the kid that this man had been. To grow up feeling so broken must have been hard. Her childhood hadn't been easy, but she had known she was loved.

Reaching across the table, she set her hand on his free one and gave it a squeeze. "I really am sorry you had to go through that."

Chad shrugged. "It's what made me who I am."

It was late afternoon by the time her dad finally called to ask for a ride. They'd immediately jumped up and headed to pick him up.

He'd been surprised to see Chad when they got there but didn't mention it. She'd seen it on his face and in the look he gave her. She ignored him and his questioning glances.

"Any chance someone would be at the gym?" Chad asked from the backseat.

"No one mentioned it, but we can check. Why?" Rich asked.

"They wouldn't let me in last night, so I don't have my keys or anything other than my phone."

"Ah" was all he said.

"I'll go by there now," she told them.

Unfortunately, it was a waste, as no one was there. Chad jumped out and tried the doors, but it seemed everything was still locked up.

"Dammit," he said when he got back in.

"I'll make some calls and see if I can find anyone to open it for you." Dad turned to Kendall. "Take us to Grady's. I'm hungry."

She nodded and pulled out of the lot. As with everything around them, it was a short drive, and she quickly pulled up in front of the pub.

They all got out and went in, heading straight for their usual table with Chad right behind them. Her dad surprised her by grabbing his usual side of the booth and then telling Kendall to scoot over and let Chad sit next to her.

The mixed signals she was getting from everyone about Chad was starting to drive her nuts. The ones she was giving herself weren't helping either.

Grady came up with a beer for Rich and sodas for Chad and Kendall. "Looks like they sprung you, huh?" It would be pointless to ask how he knew, the man knew everything.

"These kids just picked me up. You're my first stop after the big house." Rich threw back the mug of beer, drinking almost all of it in one gulp.

"I'll get you another." Grady laughed as he turned to Kendall and Chad. "Everyone having their usuals?"

They all nodded, and Grady left.

"How does he know what everyone eats?" Chad asked.

"I used to think he had notes in the back, but I've been back there and couldn't find any," Kendall teased.

"Grady never forgets a thing." Rich tapped his temple with his finger.

"Now, what good would I be if I couldn't remember my favorite customers' orders?" Grady asked as he walked back up with another mug of beer for Rich. "She telling you that she thinks I cheat?" He looked at Chad.

"Hey, that's on her," Chad laughed.

"Oh sure, just throw me under the bus while you were the one that asked the question." Kendall rolled her eyes.

"I told you, girl—I remember everything."

"I'll figure out how you do it one day," she teased him as he left.

Her dad was typing away on his phone when she turned back to him. He set it down with a thud on the table before taking a sip of his new beer.

"Tommy is going to swing by the gym to get your things and bring them here," he told Chad.

She wasn't prepared for the disappointment of him not coming back to her place to hang out. After she'd finished her articles today, they'd had a decent time together. Once she knew her dad was okay, she'd relaxed a little, still worried but not as much. It wasn't the first time he'd been locked up for a night, even if she didn't like it.

Most of the fighters she remembered being around were either the older men that she'd known forever and had acted as surrogate fathers, or were cocky younger men that had cured any desire in her life to want to be with a fighter romantically.

Chad was somehow different than both categories. He was kind, a little playful, but quiet and listened well. She'd told him stories about growing up around the rings and the boxing world, and he'd made her feel like he listened to every word she was saying.

Even now, sitting next to him at the table, she could feel the warmth coming off his body and had to actually stop herself from reaching down and putting her hand on his leg.

It was for the best, she decided, that she didn't spend more time with him outside the gym. The last thing she needed was to get involved with a fighter and end up caught in more events like last night, or so she tried to convince herself.

Chapter Eight

The gym had opened back up Thursday morning, and Chad had been here all day, prepping for his fight tonight. This fight was going to take all he had. Last time he'd won, but barely, and really only because Jimmy was already injured.

This was a weight class he'd only barely made it into, and Jimmy was easily at the top end, if not already in the next. He was sizable, and while most of the time, that didn't bother Chad, he knew what his skills were.

An octagon had been set up in the basement of the gym for these fights. It was mostly his doing financially, but he enjoyed having the opportunity to be the home fighter. The octagon would also give him a place to train without having to modify the boxing ring, and since no one else here was doing mixed martial arts style fighting, he had this all to himself.

He was supposed to have another trainer come and help him this week with his MMA skills, which would have been a great benefit before this fight, but with everything that had happened, they had backed out. Soon he'd find someone else to help him train with his takedowns and other skills, but for now, the boxing lessons from Rich were doing exactly what he needed.

"You ready?" Rich asked, stepping into the locker room.

Chad nodded even though he wasn't sure he really was. "As ready as I'll ever be."

Rich walked over and sat down on the bench across from him. "Sometimes the fights don't turn out how we want them to. Sometimes they turn out different than we expect. Every single fight is a learning opportunity if you make it one."

The man didn't seem like he would be when you first met him, but he was full of wisdom on things outside fighting. He could also keep any secret you put on him, and Chad was positive he'd take it to his grave.

"I wanted to thank you for taking care of Kendall the other night." Rich pinched the bridge of his nose. "I didn't know that McDonnell was that hotheaded, but I appreciate you keeping her out of harm's way."

"I tried my best." Chad shrugged. He hadn't done anything, really, and the fight had still spilled out into the parking lot.

"Well, it was certainly enough, and you didn't spend any time in jail," Rich joked.

"Maybe not, but that was mostly because Kendall got pissed at all the questions and basically told the cops to fuck off."

"That's my girl," he laughed. "I'll be back in just a few minutes."

Rich left, and Chad took the time to think about how he ended up here. Too many times in his life, he'd been picked on and bullied. Being a nerd wasn't helpful for social status, but he'd done a damn good job at making money.

It also helped that generally he kept a low profile, away from the public. No one had much to say about a skinny geeky-looking guy, even if he has money. As he put on muscle and changed the way he dressed, his looks had evolved, making people that had never really paid any attention to him wonder if they had ever seen him before.

Last year, he'd hired an image consultant—because apparently that was a thing—and she'd helped him buy the right clothes and say the right words, but had suggested he start working out. Then she'd gotten pissed when he decided MMA was what he wanted to do.

No one here knew who he really was except for Rich and Tommy. Tommy only knew because of the octagon. Nothing that pertained to fighting contained his last name, and that was a rule he'd set down a long time ago with Tommy and Rich. Chad had needed to come clean in order to explain he could bankroll the gym but just needed the space.

Tommy had nearly fallen out of his chair when Chad had told him. His company was worth billions, and he was worth just as much. After Tommy had recovered from his shock, he'd agreed to let Chad build the ring and to keep his secret, as long as he promised not to sue him if he got hurt.

There were a million risks involved in what he was doing, but he never considered them to be the gym's risks. Chad had gone to his lawyer, who was equally shocked, and had him draft a liability waiver on behalf of the gym and had given it to Tommy who'd been satisfied he wouldn't be sued, and the project had moved forward.

He'd also been the one to set up the security system and was helping Tommy bring his books into the twenty-first century. It helped that he knew the camera was there and was able to help Kendall not freak out when she found out Rich was in jail.

This would be the first fight in the new octagon that wasn't for training. One he didn't want to do and shouldn't have agreed to, but he didn't back down from a fight. He also understood Jimmy's need to challenge him since he'd lost the last fight.

"Look who I found," Rich announced as he walked in.

Kendall laughed from behind him as she followed him in.

Of all the people he didn't want to show up, she was at the top of the list. "What are you doing here?" he asked more brusquely than he should have.

She shot him a confused look but quickly replaced it with her smile. "I came to watch the fight." She said it simply, like this was something she did every Thursday night.

He couldn't help but wonder why she was suddenly so interested in the fighting. From everything Rich had told him about her before the first fight, he thought she'd never come around. Now she was about to watch him fight for the third time in a week.

His nerves were already all over the place, and now she was here, and it was throwing him off. He was attracted to her to say the least, but that was something he knew he could never act on or Rich would kick his ass, and he'd deserve it.

"Rich, we need you to take a look at this," someone poked their head in and called.

He didn't pay attention to who it was. He was watching Kendall and trying to pretend he wasn't.

"Why'd you agree to this?" she asked.

"To this fight? It was going to happen eventually."

She tilted her head, studying him. "Why's that?"

"Just was."

She nodded, accepting his lack of answer. "Why do you do this?" she asked after a minute.

"Do what?"

"Fight."

"Because I like it. I want to do this. Do I need another reason?" He was getting defensive now but couldn't help it. Her questions were hitting a nerve.

"I never said there was anything wrong with your answer," she told him. "Can I quote you?"

"Sure, whatever. What's with the third degree?"

"I asked you simple questions. You know what small talk is, right?" she threw back at him.

"I know what it is, but do you really think now is the right time to be chatting about the fucking weather?"

"Hey now," Rich added to the conversation. He hadn't even known Rich had come back in.

"Good luck out there. I'm going to go grab a seat." She gave him a small smile and kissed Rich on the cheek before letting herself out.

"That was a little rough," Rich commented.

"Yeah." It was, and he wasn't about to explain to Rich what was going on because he didn't know himself.

"Anything you need to tell me about you and Kendall?" he asked.

"Nope." And it was true. There was nothing he needed to say now or later because nothing was going to happen.

"All right, then."

Chad changed the subject. "What was that about?"

"Nothing important. Just Jimmy's coach wanting to make sure everything was good after the other night."

"Guess word got around pretty quickly."

Rich looked back at him for a second as though he was going to say something and then changed his mind. He checked Chad's gloves before patting him on the back. "Come on. Let's get to it."

Chad rolled his shoulders, attempting to let go of some of the tension before heading out. The crowd was small, but most of them cheered him on as he walked past.

"Get out of your head," Rich whispered.

He took a deep breath and dropped his phone onto the bench that Rich would occupy. "I'm trying."

"If you want a chance at this fight, try harder." Rich put his hands on Chad's shoulders and gave him a firm squeeze. "Size isn't everything. You've got patience and agility."

"Three rounds," Chad reminded himself. It wasn't going to be a long fight tonight. They were just testing the octagon out and the whole arena setup. Three rounds. He repeated those two words over and over as he stepped into the ring and the cage slammed shut behind him.

Chapter Nine

"We have a winner!" The referee held up Jimmy's arm as he pounded on his chest with his other.

Kendall felt worse now than she had when she'd taken her seat. She'd tried to question Chad earlier because she'd recognized he was nervous and thought maybe she could get a few good answers out of him.

That was shitty of her, and she knew it. As soon as she'd asked the first one, she'd known better, and it wasn't like she even got an answer to make it worth asking. He'd been closed off. She should have approached it yesterday when they were both at her place.

Now, not only had she been rude, but he'd lost the fight. Lost by tapping out at that, which she knew was going to serve as a major blow to his ego. It might not be that big a deal since this was a small fight as far as crowds went, but he'd feel it.

The first round had been a struggle to sit back and watch. Chad wasn't calm like he had been in the first fight she'd watched him in. He was moving a lot, and she could hear her dad yelling at him to stop.

The second round had been worse. Barely a minute into it,

Jimmy had gotten Chad onto the ground twice, and the second time had been the final one.

However, it did occur to her that she'd really know what he was made of by how he acted in the next few moments. If he was a poor sport, she'd leave it at that. No more tiptoeing around. She'd directly ask him for an interview and keep it professional.

If he was gracious, well then, she was screwed. She'd thought of nothing but him all day as she researched the sport to know more before she came tonight. She even cleaned his shorts today after calling her dad for laundry instructions on them.

Then she'd gone and left them sitting on her table at home. That was a genuine accident—it was definitely not because she wanted to see him again and needed the excuse just in case.

As she watched, Chad stood up and walked over to Jimmy to shake his hand. She was doomed. He was hot and a good sport. He had his back to her, and she enjoyed watching every muscle move each time he brought his arm up to talk to someone else.

It was making her uncomfortable to be sitting here and looking at him, so she rose and went to her dad. Next time, she'd bring her camera, though, and get some good shots for the article, if she ever wrote it.

"Hey, Dad."

"Hey, kiddo," he answered.

"He's taking this really well," she commented as she watched Chad talk to Jimmy.

He was watching them too. "Yeah. He's got a long way to go despite his talent, but he's never a sore loser."

"That's rare."

He nodded and moved back as Chad stepped out of the cage. Kendall moved to the side as well, making sure everyone had room as they exited.

Chad was watching her—she could feel it. When she turned to look at him, he didn't pretend he wasn't looking, and there was a flash in his eyes of something—desire maybe—that was so quick, she wasn't sure if she really saw it.

She shook her head. There was no way that was what she saw, especially after he was short with her earlier and had just lost. Surely there was some pent-up aggression in him that didn't involve lust for her. She was imagining what she wanted to be there, was all.

"You did all right," her dad was saying.

"No, I didn't," Chad admitted. "I was too in my head over his size alone that I couldn't even make a good move. I was waiting for him to take me down, and he did."

"I didn't say you did great," her dad clarified.

"No one ever accused you of that," Chad laughed.

"Come on. Let's head back to the locker room and get ready to head home. Nothing more can be done about it tonight."

Kendall followed. She hadn't really been invited to do so, but she didn't know what else to do with herself. When they reached the locker room door, she hung back, planning to stay outside and wait for her dad to come out.

"Come on," he told her.

"I can wait out here. No need for me to follow you in," she assured him.

"It's fine," Chad yelled from inside.

"Okay, then." Awkwardly, she let herself in and walked over to the far wall.

"It's done now," Chad was saying. "I'm not fighting him again. He got to prove he could take me, and that's it for me."

"You might change your mind later, but I agree—for now, that's it."

"I need to find another trainer still, so I might take tomorrow off."

"That's not a bad idea," Rich agreed. "This week has been pig shit, so we can wait until Monday to pick back up. I think we all deserve a break. I'm going to go home and plant my ass in my recliner for the whole weekend."

"Hey!" Kendall joked. "You are supposed to be coming over for dinner this weekend."

"Well, I might get up for that, but that's it," he teased. "You should come too," he told Chad.

"I couldn't impose on you guys." He backed out as the same man who had done it before came in and started to take off his gloves and unwrap his hands.

"It's not a problem. Come on over, Saturday around six," Kendall told him against her own best judgment.

"If you're sure it's not an imposition?"

"It's not."

"Can I bring anything?" he offered, flexing his hands now that they were free.

She shook her head. "I'll have everything. I'm cooking, so I guess I better go to the grocery store so it's not yogurt night."

Chad laughed. "How is that the only thing in your fridge?"

"I don't need as many calories as someone who's training."

"Fair enough."

"I'll see you two then. I'm going to head home. I've got some work to do." After kissing her dad on his cheek, she let herself out.

The drive home was quiet save for the million things running around in her head now. Chad wasn't what she expected, and she needed to decide what to do with that information.

She also needed to write an article about him. Technically, he'd given her permission to use his nonanswers earlier, but she knew that was a stretch, since he hadn't been paying attention.

It was also confusing that he seemed surprised she'd asked questions. He knew she was a journalist, so even if he didn't yet know she wanted to write about him, he should've realized she was going to ask a lot of questions.

Well, she hoped he knew that. Surely her dad had told him why she was coming around, or at least what she did for a living. Someone had to have told him, then again, it wasn't like she had brought it up at any point.

Sitting down with her laptop, she decided she'd write about tonight instead of just Chad. She'd use his name this time but be sure to leave out the last name, which she didn't know anyway, to help keep his identity a secret, since she didn't have real buy-in from him.

It was a vague enough name that she should be able to leave it at that. Plus, if he truly didn't know what she did, he wouldn't see the articles. He hadn't mentioned the other one, but then she didn't talk to him much about his fights.

It was such a hard place to be sitting in. She knew what she needed to do, and she was going to do it. But she wanted more from him and not just when it came to the article. She was screwed.

Chapter Ten

She spent all day on this next article. She was now ahead on her work, having already submitted two, but her goal was to stay that way, then if there was a lull, she'd have some grace time.

Writing this article had taken a lot out of her though. The first article using his name was covering a loss, but she tried to spin it positively while also being accurate about the details.

Her morning was spent debating if she should even write the article. The afternoon was spent deciding how to do it. In the end, she decided not to use his name yet. She hoped it wasn't dragging out the mystery of who he was too far, or her boss would be pissed.

For better or worse, she closed her laptop and headed to the office, somewhere she hadn't been much this week, just to show face as she submitted it.

Sindee had texted her all week, and she'd barely replied with everything else going on. She did send her the article for the sake of trying to explain about the fight.

Sindee had replied within minutes, demanding the full story

from her. Kendall had put her off until today, talking her into a girls' night instead.

The office was humming with activity as it always was on a Friday. With the latest paper coming out tomorrow, it was always a scramble. There was an edition on Wednesdays, but not everyone had articles in it. It was a much smaller version of the Saturday edition.

"Kendall!" Robert yelled for her almost as soon as she stepped in.

Slowly, she made her way to his office. It was so hard to tell with him if it was going to be good news or bad.

"Afternoon, Robert," she said as she stepped into his office.

"Close the door," he told her without looking up from his computer.

Kendall closed the door with a soft click and then took a seat.

"Why are we not revealing the fighter's identity in this article?"

"I didn't think it was best to do that on a loss."

"For who? The fighter or the public?"

"Both." She added as much confidence as she could to her statement, hoping he'd not see through it to the fact that she was more worried about the man than the readers.

He stared her down so long she had to fight the urge to squirm. "Fine. That's probably for the best, but the next article needs a signed media release and a photo. We don't clickbait, and I won't continue to do it for you."

Nothing he said should surprise her, but that did. She also didn't think he knew what clickbait meant, since the articles were in the actual paper and not online.

"Yes, sir," she answered.

"Good. Now go get me that article."

Kendall nodded and left his office quickly, heading for her desk where Sindee was already waiting.

"What was that about?" she asked.

"He doesn't want me to tease out who he is anymore."

"Do you have a release from him yet?"

Kendall shook her head. If she didn't get one, she'd be screwed, so hopefully he didn't mind. That was a lot of pressure on one hope. Damn.

"I'm still coming over tonight, right?"

Kendall nodded. "That's the plan. Drinks and movies?"

"And a huge story to tell me about," Sindee laughed as she walked to her own desk.

For her part, Kendall pulled out her phone and messaged her dad.

Kendall: Do you think you can set up some time with Chad for an interview?

Rich: I can set up a meeting.

Kendall: Fine, whatever you want to call it.

Rich: Where?

Kendall: How about here? I can use the conference room and make it an official interview.

Rich: When?

Kendall: Let's do tomorrow if there's time?

Rich: I'll let you know.

She resisted the urge to scream in frustration and dropped her phone into her purse. Her dad was particularly short on words today, and that didn't help.

Chad had to agree. Why wouldn't he? It was a great opportunity to get his name out there and get recognition. He had to want it.

There was something about him, though, that made her wonder if he did. He didn't seem impressed even when he won, and he didn't gloat at all. He looked proud for himself but mostly, in the two whole fights she'd seen him win, he did only what he had to before retreating to the locker room.

His behavior stood out to her because most of the fighters in either sport she'd seen were pumped up and excited to have won. He just looked accomplished and tired.

If he had sought out her dad to train him then he had to want more. Why else would you look for someone and insist they train you?

"You ready to head out?" Sindee asked.

"Yeah, let's get out of here."

Her dad hadn't texted back, and she wondered if Chad had declined. Biting her lip, she picked up her bag and walked out with Sindee.

"So, booze first?" Sindee's laugh echoed in the hallway.

"Once I go home, I am not going back out again, so booze and food?"

"I love the way you think."

They both drove their own cars to the grocery store and grabbed the alcohol and frozen pizzas before heading back to Kendall's. Despite her compulsive need to check her phone now, she hadn't heard back from her dad.

"Earth to Kendall." Sindee waved a piece of pizza in her face.

"Sorry." She grabbed the slice and took a bite.

"Got anything to do with that fighter you've been hanging with?"

"I'm just so worried he won't accept an interview."

"Sleep with him." Sindee shrugged as Kendall choked on her pizza.

"I am not going to sleep with him for a damn article."

"But you would for other reasons? Do tell." Sindee leaned forward and grinned.

"What are we, teenagers?"

"You can pretend to be if it gets you to tell me what's been going on."

Kendall rolled her eyes but launched into the story of her week. It was hard to believe with everything that had happened that it had been less than a week.

"So, wait—you're telling me that he stayed the night and slept on the floor of your living room and nothing happened at all?"

Kendall nodded. She had been the one to fall asleep first that night anyway.

"Man's a saint. There's no other excuse."

"Not everyone is constantly thinking about sex, Sindee."

She shrugged. "Their loss, then."

"Well, I was a little worried about my dad," Kendall reminded her.

"Why? Of all the people I've ever met in my life, I would say that your dad could handle himself."

"Be that as it may, I was worried when I hadn't heard from him. Then we found out the next day that he was in jail."

"And completely fine."

She shot Sindee a look. "It's been a long freaking week."

"All jokes aside, how is Rich holding up?"

"He seemed fine, honestly. I haven't had a chance to talk to him much, though, except I messaged him earlier, trying to get him to set up a meeting with Chad for me so I could interview him, but I never heard back."

"Oh, sweetie." Sindee set her drink down and looked at her. "Don't you think you should have been the one to ask him?"

"Why?" Kendall tilted her head, confused. Their whole conversation had been to do with her dad in one way or another, so it seemed appropriate.

"Because if he genuinely doesn't know you're a reporter, then he's going to be pissed off."

She thought it over. If he really didn't know, then asking him for an interview herself wasn't going to change anything. Just then, her phone went off.

"Hey, Dad," she answered.

"Chad said he's in, but it will have to be in the afternoon."

"I can make that work."

"Ask him!" Sindee whispered.

"Does he know why I want to meet?"

"Nope. Seemed confused. Wasn't my place to tell him."

"Dad!" She fussed. Why didn't he tell him? "You never told him what I do or why I was there?"

"Didn't come up." She could hear the shrug in his voice.

"This is going to be lovely." Rolling her eyes, she pinched the bridge of her nose as she fought back the headache that was threatening.

"I'll be there about two. He said he'd be a little later."

"You're coming?" she asked.

"Oh, I wouldn't miss this for anything."

"Damn." She hung up the phone and looked over at Sindee who was struggling to contain her laughter.

"Want that drink now?" Sindee asked.

"That one and maybe a few more."

Chapter Eleven

Chad had wracked his brain last night for any reason that Kendall had asked for a meeting with him that didn't involve her knowing who he really was and had come up short. Stressed was an understatement.

This morning he did what any sensible person who wasn't thinking with his dick would do: he searched her on the internet. That had led to his current state of anger and confusion as he pulled up to the address that Rich had given him.

To his shock and horror, it was the newspaper office. He called his lawyer as soon as he put his car in Park.

"I'm going to need you to keep an eye on the paper for anything about me. I am not agreeing to an interview or a photo session," he said as soon as his lawyer picked up.

"Hello to you, too. That is both incredibly vague and very specific. Are you angling for my job?" he joked.

"I'm not fucking kidding."

"Doesn't sound like you are. What happened? The chick you've got the hots for turn out to be a reporter?"

Chad didn't say a word and waited for him to realize he was right.

"Oh shit. No freaking way."

"If you don't fucking quit goofing off. I don't know why I bothered to hire you. Always joking around."

"Not always. And you hired me because you like me and I make you laugh. It's all about the charm."

"No, I hired you because you're supposed to be good at what you do."

"I am."

"Whatever. I have to go."

"I'm billing you for this call."

"Of course you are," Chad mumbled.

He got out of his car and slammed the door shut as he walked up to the office doors.

Kendall was waiting there to greet him. "Hey. Thanks for coming. Follow me."

She was dressed to kill today. In the little time he'd known her, he'd never seen her so put together, or with so much makeup on.

Her curves filled out her fitted dress in ways that left little to his imagination, and he had to admit, he'd imagined it a few times. The black dress was complemented by red heels and a black-and-red blazer.

The makeup was a different story. He liked her better at the gym, natural with comfy clothes on. It looked good, but it didn't look like her.

Kendall didn't look comfortable either. Wearing heels wasn't her strong suit, and he could see it, but only because he was watching her so hard as she led him to a conference room.

Rich sat to the back of the room near the windows that lined the entire far wall. The room was sparse. A few water bottles had been set out, but other than that and a long black table and black chairs, the only other thing in here was a huge TV on the wall.

Rich was on the phone and held up one finger, telling him to wait as he finished the call. Chad took a seat and grabbed one of the bottles of water, downing it as they waited.

"I have good news," Rich said as he walked up.

"What's that?" Chad asked.

"I've got you an MMA fight for next weekend. It's with an out-of-towner, but he's close to you in weight. We need to look him up when we get home."

He pulled out a chair next to Chad and took a seat. Across from them, Kendall clicked her pen repeatedly as she looked down at a blank notebook.

Resigned, he interlaced his fingers and rested his elbows on the table. "What's this about?" he asked, needing her to tell him and prove he was right.

"I was hoping we could mutually benefit each other."

Chad arched a brow at her. The sales pitch had begun. "How's that?"

"Well, I'm the sports reporter here, and I was hoping to get you to agree to an interview and a few photos."

"No," he answered, not needing to hear anything else.

"It would be good for your career too. It's not a big paper, but it would get you some recognition. I promise I have zero intent of screwing you over with it and am happy to give you the final approval on the article itself."

He shook his head and went to stand up, only to be stopped by Rich's hand on his shoulder. "Hear her out, please?"

He sent a glare to Kendall but relaxed back into his seat.

"I'm going to level with you. I didn't want to be the sports journalist here, but it's a good job, and I can't afford to lose it. I really have no intention of writing about you negatively, I promise. You can look at the other articles I've done on the fights and see for yourself."

"Other articles?"

Kendall nodded. "Just articles. I haven't used your name, and no photos."

He had screwed up. He couldn't remember the last time he hadn't done at least a cursory check on the people he kept company with, but he hadn't even tried with her at all. He'd assumed she was just hovering around her dad, but it turned out that it was all for a story.

"The articles are actually very popular. People love to read about the fights. I got a few letters today asking who you were. I haven't answered them, I promise. Hell, I don't even know who you are, really."

It was going to stay that way. He looked over at Rich to confirm she didn't know who he was.

Rich gave his head a small shake. "I keep my personal and work life separate," he assured him.

"That's funny, Rich. I'm pretty sure your personal life just collided hard with your work life." Chad cocked his head toward Kendall. "It'd be a hell of a scoop for your daughter the reporter, wouldn't it?"

"Hey now—watch your tone with me."

It nearly worked. He felt himself about to lean back and accept that Rich had told him what to do. Instead, he leaned forward and took a look around the room.

"I can't believe I trusted you and thought you were trying to be there for your dad. All along the two of you had been planning an ambush?"

Kendall shook her head and reached out for his hands. He pulled them off the table and forced both hands to remain in his lap.

"I promise it isn't like that," she said.

Chapter Twelve

C had's jaw was clenched so hard, she wondered if he'd chip a tooth. This wasn't going well, and she tried to rein it back in.

"I just want to showcase all that you're doing. I can't guarantee it would really do anything for your career, but it would be a great thing to have on the wall at the gym. The paper is small, but people are really following your story."

"What story?" he asked through his gritted teeth.

"Like I said, there have been other articles. I've not taken any pictures, and I definitely didn't use any names or anything. But I built up to maybe revealing who you were." She added the last part with an apologetic look.

"Maybe you should have fucking asked me first before writing articles about me."

"I genuinely thought you knew what I did until I found out last night from Dad that you didn't." She cut her eyes to her dad. "There was no reason for me to assume that you didn't know or that Dad hadn't told you why I was coming around."

She could see the tight string that was his anger coming undone. He was holding it in, but soon that string was going to snap.

"Look, it's important to me and my career, but I can't force you, I know that. I'm confused and a little hurt that you don't trust me with the article even after the assurances I've given you, but that's your decision, and I will do what I can to respect it."

"Do what you can?" Chad stood up. "What the hell is that supposed to mean?"

"Sit down, son," her dad urged him.

"Son? No. This is bullshit. You've been setting me up for this?"

"I didn't set you up for anything."

"You did. Clear as day, you invited your daughter out to write about me."

"I invited her out to write about the fights, not about you specifically."

"Do you have any fucking idea what will happen if people find out that it's me?" Chad demanded.

He remained rooted to the spot in front of his chair as he yelled at her dad. It was as though he'd completely forgotten she was there.

"Do you?" her dad countered.

"That damn image consultant was right, this was a bad idea. I wanted to improve my fucking image, not have people think I am going to fight them. I need to stay under wraps, and I thought you understood that." His tone changed subtly with the last sentence. He sounded hurt, and she wished she had never started this path with the articles.

"I'm sorry. I will find someone else to write about who wants to do it. I really believed you would want the exposure, but I screwed up." Shifting all the blame back to herself, she stood up and stared him down. "I don't know what your story is, and I won't ask you for it again, that I can promise—but you are not going to stand in here and yell at my father like that—I don't care who you are. He went to jail over your fucking fight, so if you want to be mad at someone, then you can be mad at me. Otherwise, shut up and quit acting like a toddler having a temper tantrum."

She didn't know where the sudden burst of bravery came from, but she was proud of herself. He was being an ass. Even if he was blindsided, this was ridiculous.

"A child, am I? You two fucking tricked me." He turned to leave and knocked the chair over in the process. It wasn't hard to recognize his indecision in the split second he debated picking it back up before he left it and the room.

"What the hell was that about, Dad?" she demanded, turning to him.

"I can't tell you anything."

"I'm not going to write about him."

"I can't tell you on or off the record."

"You could have told me he wouldn't want this. At any time, you could have said that to me. You could have told him what I do and why I was there. Now I'm screwed, he's mad at both of us, and I can't do shit about it."

He studied her as she dropped back into the chair. "You can always do something about it."

"No. There's not a single chance in hell that he would ever talk to me again."

"I think you're wrong."

"It doesn't matter what you think. It is what it is."

The worst part was she didn't blame Chad for being upset or feeling like he'd been tricked. That hadn't been her intent, but she understood why he thought it.

Slowly, she gathered the few things she had brought into the conference room and put them in her bag.

"Kiddo, he'll come around."

"No, he won't. This was wrong. I don't know what he's hiding, but I feel like shit for asking him for it. If I had known, Dad, I never would have started down that path. That's my fault, and maybe it's another reason why I'm not cut out for this job."

"It doesn't have anything to do with that. He needs to get his head out of his ass and see that this isn't a bad thing. You need to fight for what you want."

He stood up and pushed his chair in before picking up the one Chad had knocked over and pushing it in too.

"There's nothing to fight here. It shouldn't always be a battle. Sometimes it's just about respect."

"Respect goes both ways."

"We literally ambushed him."

"No, he saw it that way, but we didn't. From the beginning, you let him know disclosing his identity is his decision."

"It doesn't matter how any of us saw it. The only thing that does matter is that he's hurt and offended by it, and I can't fix that."

"Here." He handed her a small piece of paper.

"What's this?" She reached out and took it from him.

"It's Chad's number in case you decide he is worth a fighting chance."

"Dad," she sighed even as she put it in her bag.

"I'm going to head out. Call me if you need anything."

"Probably a place to live," she muttered.

"You'll come up with something. Write about someone else."

"I'll call you if there's anything I need."

He gave her a stiff nod and let himself out of the conference room as well. She remained in her seat and dropped her head into her hands. She was screwed.

She'd been worried about how he'd react all morning, but this didn't even come close. The journalist in her was sure he'd agree and was ready to meet any sort of demand he had for the article. The woman in her was worried he'd hate her.

This scenario wasn't one she had thought of. Reaching back into her bag, she opened the paper and pulled out his number. For half a second, she thought about calling.

Now wasn't the time to worry about him. Even if he was going to forgive her, it wouldn't be today, and it wouldn't happen at all until he cooled off. She needed to worry about herself now, and her job.

She pulled the notebook back out and one of her colorful pens. It was time to think of literally anything else she could write about.

Listing everything helped and left her feeling at least somewhat accomplished. She had a few places to start and was ready to get things moving along.

If Chad wouldn't let her write about him, she'd make something else more interesting. Hopefully, Robert and the readers would buy it, though she wasn't sure if she did.

During the drive home, she thought of her next steps. She also thought of Chad and the look of straight-up betrayal he'd had on his face today.

When she got home, she poured herself a glass of wine and curled up in her bed with her laptop. Tomorrow she'd do the things. Today she'd feel bad about screwing it all up.

She shook her head though. One thing was sitting with her. What did he mean by image consultant?

Chapter Thirteen

He'd cooled off for a few days but was finally back in the gym on Wednesday after a long talk with Rich. The older man had apologized for not being up front and tried to get him to talk to Kendall too.

Kendall was a different story. He wasn't ready to forgive and forget even though he recognized he had been an asshole on Saturday.

Training had started out slow today and was picking up in intensity when he felt the air change in the room. As though he had conjured her up from thin air just by thinking about her, Kendall walked into the gym.

Her eyes sought him out from across the wide, open space, and she held his gaze for just a second before looking away. No matter to him—he was back to focusing on his workout, getting ready for a boxing sparring match later.

Focus was something he'd rarely struggled with before she'd come into his life, but now he couldn't think straight. She needed to find a new story, fast, and get the hell back out of the gym.

She walked around the gym for an hour and chatted with several different people. They all seemed excited to talk to her, and she had her phone out for each person as though she was interviewing them for real.

The longer she stayed, the more frustrated he got. If she wouldn't leave him alone about this story on her own, then he'd make sure she understood he was off-limits.

With a thud, he dropped the weights he'd barely been using and walked over to her. "What are you doing here?"

"Trying to save my job." She didn't look up at him, but clicked her phone off and set it down on the bench she was currently occupying.

"I told you I don't want any articles."

"I didn't come here to ask you for one."

"Nope, you never did that."

"I am not writing about you. If you need proof, I'll send Dad my next article before it goes to print. Hint taken. Now leave me alone as I have you."

"Find something else to write about," he told her.

"I have permission to be here." She looked up at him calmly. "I am not leaving, but I will leave you alone. Best I can do."

"Best you can do? What the fuck is that supposed to mean?"

"I'm still going to write about the fighting world. You can't stop me. You don't own the press."

The fact that he *could* own the press crossed his mind briefly. He could buy it right now and demand she never write about him or the fights again. That wouldn't solve shit, so he let the thought fly past.

"It's dangerous here," he reminded her. "I'm not going to be there to save your ass next time."

"It wasn't my ass that needed saving. It was yours, or you could have gone to jail, too, or worse." She stood up, jabbing a finger at him as she spoke. "McDonnell was after you, not me."

"Go interview him then!" he yelled back at her.

"I don't want to interview him!"

They stood there for a moment, both of them letting their anger get the best of them before Rich came between them. "That's enough. Nothing to see here, everyone. Carry on."

Everyone? It wasn't until then that he realized their whole exchange was being watched by everyone at the gym.

They'd been louder than he thought if they'd attracted this much notice. Damn.

"You need to go get ready," Rich told him.

"She needs to go," Chad countered.

"I'm not making her leave as long as she isn't writing about you. Tommy told her the same thing, so go on."

He shot one last look at Kendall before walking away. She got on his nerves. Hell, he got on his own nerves right now.

Despite the fact that he was mad at her and felt used, he still wanted to sleep with her, and that only served to fuel his anger. Attraction was a powerful thing, and he'd seen it land more than one person he knew in loads of trouble. He wasn't falling for it.

What he was going to do was get trashed at a bar tonight and, hopefully, get laid. He'd erase her from his mind one way or another.

An hour later, he was walking out to the ring, only to see Kendall standing right next to it, talking to Hugh, his sparring opponent. Hugh was all smiles and seemed to be telling her a story.

As Chad approached them, Kendall kept her eyes away from him. He didn't bother to pretend he wasn't watching her, which wouldn't serve any purpose since damn near everyone in here had been a witness to their argument earlier.

Her genuine laughter drifted over him, and he struggled to keep his cock from getting hard. She'd wormed her way into everything around him and he missed her even while mad at her. Hearing her laugh that he missed had his body betraying him. He bounced around the ring some, warming up his muscles as he watched Kendall and Hugh continue to chat.

Hugh reached out to touch her shoulder, and Chad decided enough was enough. He wasn't going to sit here and watch her flirt with another fighter.

"You done fucking around yet?" he threw at Hugh.

"Not by a long shot," Hugh answered but climbed into the ring anyway. "What the fuck is your problem?"

"Don't have one."

"Right." Hugh rolled his shoulders as Tommy stepped into the ring.

"I'm your ref for the evening, gentlemen. Play nice, and remember, this is just a spar."

From the corner of his eye, Chad watched as Kendall walked around the ring and took a seat. It appeared she was here for the show tonight too.

A conversation with Tommy was long overdue at this point, but it would have to wait until after the match. Then he'd explain that Kendall needed to go.

They were well into the second round when he got a good hit in to Hugh's face. "What the fuck, man?"

"It's a legal hit," Chad told him.

"Yeah, but this is supposed to be a spar."

"If you can't handle it, then leave."

Their conversation continued as they circled each other in the center of the ring.

"Is this about the chick?" Hugh grinned, finally clueing himself in to what was happening.

"No, it's not about her. This is a fight."

"This is emotional investment, and I didn't sign up for that shit. If she's your girl, then all you had to do was say something."

"She's not my girl." Chad advanced on Hugh and got one off to his ribs.

"Then you wouldn't care if I asked her out tonight?" Hugh taunted.

"Go for it. She's trouble."

"Hey, Kendall," Hugh yelled.

That was it. That was all it took to take the match from any semblance of friendly to straight rage. Chad saw red and took advantage of the moment when Hugh was preoccupied and advanced on him.

Chad threw punch after punch as he trapped Hugh in the far corner, away from Kendall.

"That's enough!" Tommy yelled as he attempted to separate them.

"Knock it off!" It was Rich's yell that got him to step back.

"What the hell?" Hugh yelled as he climbed out of the ring.

"I don't know what's wrong with you, but you know better than to act like that," Rich said as he came up behind him.

"Whatever."

"No. Not whatever. If you're going to act like that, then I'm done. I don't know what happened between you two, but it better never happen again."

Truth be told, he didn't know what his problem was either. He'd never been very jealous and especially not about someone he wasn't even remotely seeing. There was no excuse for him tonight other than the fact that she was getting under his skin.

He didn't look at Rich, or Kendall, or anyone else as he headed to the locker room. No one spoke as he changed and got ready to leave. He didn't need to be here anymore tonight.

The second he was dressed again, he headed right for the door. Without acknowledging anyone, he slammed out and headed for his car. He needed a drink and to wash her from his mind.

Chapter Fourteen

She had spent the Thursday and most of Friday debating on going to the fight. For some reason, Robert had accepted her stories about the other fighters instead of Chad, with minimal yelling and she'd never been more grateful in her life.

Robert had been clear that all she'd done was buy herself more time. She still needed to come up with the article about the main fighter. She was screwed but had a job as long as she could continue to stall.

Tonight there were a few fights scheduled, and she'd been working herself up to going. They were happening at Tommy's gym, so it wasn't like she needed to go far. She just didn't want to run into Chad again.

Her emotions flared each time she saw him or thought of him, and she wasn't sure she had it under control yet. She needed this, she reminded herself every time she thought of backing out.

The current plan was to stay for the first two fights and leave before Chad's. It was the best option she had right now to still get a story and not watch him.

She knew she was wrong for it, but she still wanted him. Her body betrayed her whenever he was near, and it was like she lost all form of rational thought.

"Do you want me to go with you?" Sindee offered.

The thought of Sindee, all prim and proper, in there with a bunch of fighters, watching these cage fights had her cracking up. "No, thanks," Kendall managed to say despite her laughter.

"Well, damn. I didn't think it was that funny." Sindee folded her arms across her chest and pouted.

"I'm sorry. It's really not a place I think you'd enjoy."

"Whatever. You better get ready."

"I am ready." She cocked her head and looked at Sindee, confused.

"You aren't going to at least fix your hair?"

Kendall brought her hand up to the messy bun that was holding her curls back. What was wrong with her hair? "I don't think you understand where I am going."

"I don't think you understand how much you still have the hots for the unnamed fighter, and you might want to look your best."

"That ship sailed," Kendall assured her.

"Did it though? I feel like it's still in the dock."

Kendall rolled her eyes and got up to go take a look at herself. She didn't think she looked bad. She looked like she was going to go hang out at a gym and watch men fight each other.

"You know what? If you want to come, why not?" Kendall told Sindee as she went back into the living room.

"I think I might enjoy it. Sweaty, half-naked men—what's not to love?"

"You're overdressed," Kendall told her.

"Never overdressed. I am simply being me."

"You're going to stand out," Kendall told her.

"Honey, that's always my plan." Sindee winked at her as she stood up, adjusting her tight red skirt as she did.

"Let's go, then."

She had to admit, it was comforting to have Sindee there with her even if she was distracting literally every man in the place.

"Sindee! Kendall!" Grady greeted them both as he walked in.

"Grady, how are you?" Sindee gave him her best, most flirtatious smile.

"Charmed, as always, Miss Sindee." He grinned back at her. "Didn't take you for one that would be at these events."

"I am expanding my horizons and supporting my friend." Sindee leaned forward and pretended to whisper. "And I heard the views are amazing this time of year."

It took Grady a moment to recover before he burst out in laughter. "I'm sure you'll enjoy them." Still laughing, he held out his arm for Sindee to take and led her down into the basement.

"Don't mind me. I'll just follow along," Kendall muttered.

"What was that?" Sindee turned her head back and asked.

"Nothing."

They took their seats, Sindee between her and Grady, and waited for the fights to start. Sindee flirted with everyone, and Grady enjoyed the attention though it was completely harmless between them. It annoyed Kendall tonight, though, as everyone was constantly looking their way, and she thought what a bad idea it had been to bring Sindee.

There would be no hiding from Chad if she stayed long enough to see him fight. Sindee would command the attention. Great, now she was jealous of something that hadn't even happened yet.

"Mind if I join you?" Hugh asked, taking the seat next to her.

"Not at all. Wasn't sure you'd be coming out tonight."

"Eh, no hard feelings against the man. I may have provoked him a little."

Kendall giggled, imagining that he had.

"Who's this?" Sindee leaned forward and looked around Kendall to see Hugh.

With a sigh, she introduced them and then sat between them as they chatted. It was awkward, to say the least.

"Umm, is that John?" Sindee asked.

"Where?" She looked in the direction Sindee was staring and saw him. "What the fuck?"

"Pretend he isn't there. It pisses him off," Sindee told her.

"Who? The Dick-Tracy-looking dude?" Hugh asked.

Kendall snorted and nodded. It was an apt description of John who had taken every stereotype of a reporter and rolled it into one outfit tonight.

"He wants Kendall's job."

"Really?" Hugh looked down at her to confirm.

Kendall nodded. "He's also chauvinistic and annoying as hell."

"Well, if you still want it, I'm up for an interview, and maybe Sindee can snap a few photos."

"Oh, I'd love to," Sindee agreed. "Photos are great when the subject matter is as handsome as you are. Might save a few for myself."

"Okay!" Kendall stood up. "I can't listen to this shit anymore. Switch seats." She motioned for Sindee to slide over.

Taking Sindee's seat, Kendall leaned back and looked at her watch. Only ten minutes until tonight's fights started.

"You know, I'm starting to think she isn't going to run away with me one day," Grady said, knocking his shoulder into hers.

"Oh my God. Do you want to switch seats too?"

"I'm joking," he laughed before turning to look at her. "What happened with you and Chad? I thought the two of you were hitting it off at the pub the other day."

She groaned. "I screwed it up."

"So? Fix it."

"If only it were that easy."

John walked up and stood right in front of her, waiting for her to acknowledge him. When she didn't, he cleared his throat. "Robert sent me to make sure you're actually trying to get the story, and if you can't, then I will. Looks like you're just over here, goofing off instead of trying. Maybe I will score the article that Robert's been looking for since you seem unable to follow through."

"You know the fight hasn't started, right?" she asked him.

"Well aware of that."

"Then you know there's nothing to see yet?" She made her tone slightly more questioning than it needed to be just to annoy him.

Tommy stood in the cage as the fight got ready to start. "Ladies and gentlemen."

"Better grab a seat so you can watch," Grady told John, dismissing him.

"Thank you," Kendall whispered as John huffed and walked away.

"Can't stand him," Grady told her.

The fight began, and Kendall watched intently as the two fighters went all three rounds. Unfortunately, it was very one-sided, and though the second fighter hadn't been knocked out, the other was the very clear winner.

"That was a mess," Grady told her.

She nodded and turned to see what Sindee had thought of it, only to find her engrossed in a conversation with Hugh. Kendall shrugged. At least Sindee had found something to entertain her tonight.

The second fight was much better with the first two rounds going pretty much head-to-head from what she could see. And then one fighter managed to pin the other for a tap out about halfway through the third fight.

The audience had grown in the time she'd been sitting there. She'd have no problem slipping out into the crowd now.

"Weren't think of running off, were you?" Grady asked.

"I, umm," she stammered.

"You were about to get situated to watch your dad's fighter, right?"

She slumped back into her seat. "Yes." She pouted.

"That's what I thought. You always were a good kid."

Fighting Chance

Now she was stuck. She technically could still walk away, but Grady would give her that look like he was disappointed in her, and then she'd feel bad all night.

John was also here, and there was no way he was covering the main fight and she wasn't. Determined now, she sat back up and waited for the fighters to enter the octagon.

Chapter Fifteen

C had felt her again as he entered the octagon. He made it a point not to look around for her. Realizing she was still there was enough to distract him without knowing where she was watching him from.

He wanted to look though. Wanted to know who she was sitting with and if she had a good view.

Instead, he did his best to force her from his mind and concentrate on the fight. Tonight's fight was an even match, he thought, knowing the skill and size of the other man.

He managed to keep thoughts of Kendall away during it until he had pinned the other man in the third round and looked up to see her cheering him on. *God, she is beautiful* was all he could think.

It was just enough distraction for the other man to reverse the hold and get Chad pinned. He was able to get out, but wasn't able to pin him again. The match came down to points, and Chad was declared the winner.

He looked out into the crowd as the ref declared him the winner and didn't see Kendall anywhere. She had been sitting next to Grady, but that seat was now empty.

He should have been grateful she wasn't there anymore, but now he wondered why she'd left and where she'd gone. Damn her.

As soon as he could, he headed back to the locker room. He absolutely hated the attention after fights.

What people didn't understand was that he didn't do it for that. He did to prove to himself that he could—nothing else. Well, not nothing else. He also enjoyed it.

"Hi, Chad," Kendall greeted him as he entered the locker room.

He groaned. This wasn't where he thought she might have gone. "What do you want?"

"I want to talk to you." She stayed immobile, her back to the mirrors as she watched him walk over to the bench. "Congrats on winning the fight tonight."

"Thanks." What had he done to deserve this special torture of wanting the one woman that he'd also decided was completely off-limits?

"I need to tell you something," she said, breaking the silence.

"What?" He leaned forward, resting his elbows on his knees and looking at the ground.

"I have a colleague out there. I didn't know he was coming tonight, or ever, I swear. He hates me and wants the job I have, so he might try to harass you, and I just wanted you to know that I had nothing to do with it."

Chad sat up and looked at her. "Fine, you're absolved of all wrongdoings. Is that all?"

She bit her lip and shook her head. "Will you at least tell me why you're so opposed to the article?" She held up both hands to show him they were empty. "Off the record, I swear it."

"I don't need to have a reason to tell you no."

"Fine. Then let me interview you?"

"No." It was harsher than he intended, but she was wearing on him.

"Please? I swear I'll never ask again. It would also be a great way to get some exposure and make your name known."

"Dammit, Kendall." He stood up and started pacing. "When are you going to figure it out? I'm not doing an interview for you. Not now, not later, not ever."

"Why not?" she threw back at him.

"I don't want to."

"So, all that stuff you told Dad the other day, did you make it up? About your business and the image consultant, were you just making it up?"

Had he seriously admitted to the image consultant in front of her? Damn. "I never said it wasn't true. I don't need to justify myself to you, now or later. The answer is just no."

"Are you scared, then?" she asked.

"What? No. Where do you get off, accusing me of anything? I don't want to do it. It's that simple."

"No, it's not. If you want to grow at this, you're going to need to get your name out there. Unless you're scared of that, but that seems odd to me. Instead, you're just arguing in circles with me over one damn article for no reason."

"You don't know the first thing about me."

"Whose fault is that?" she asked, bringing her hands to her hips. "You know what I do, now. You are scared. You are terrified that I am right. I start publishing stories about you with your name and picture, and people will notice you. You're scared to lose fights, so you stick down here with the people who didn't make it and make sure you're rarely really challenged."

His jaw dropped. "I literally just lost. You were there!" he shouted.

"That was a one-off, and you know it. You fought him before when he was already injured, knowing you'd win. Then he challenged you back, and you had no choice but to accept. You should never have accepted the first fight even knowing he was injured."

"Wow, tell me how you really feel. If I'm such a shit fighter and person, why do you even want to interview me?"

"I never said you were shit. I said you were a coward."

He'd had enough. "Get out."

He was breathing harder now than he had in the fight. Worked up, he went to the locker room door and yanked it open to point outside. He didn't need to speak again. She knew exactly what he was telling her.

She huffed and stared him down, hands still on her hips. "Fine. Do what you want and live in secret, but don't blame anyone but yourself when you get nowhere."

"I never claimed I was trying to go anywhere with it. Did it ever occur to you that maybe this is what I wanted? That maybe I have a life outside of this gym that I didn't want merged with this one?" He paused, and when she didn't respond, he motioned for her to leave again. "I can see the answer is no. Leave."

"You know, maybe I would know these things if you had told me at some point."

"Leave," he repeated.

She stared him down but eventually walked out. Chad released the door as she did, letting it come to a satisfying click as it closed.

Frustrated, he balled his fist and stopped just short of punching the lockers. He still wanted her, and it seemed nothing was going to work to get her out of his system.

He'd even tried going to the bar the other night, but it had proved a fruitless exercise. Nothing had taken her from his mind. Not even the cute blonde that had been more than willing to assist. She did nothing for him, and he went home alone.

"You done?" Rich asked as he walked in.

"Done with what?" he snapped.

"Arguing with my daughter," Rich quipped with a grin.

"She just needs to stay gone. Why do you even let her come around after what happened the other night?" Someone needed to think of her safety.

Rich let out a small laugh. "You have met her, right? Do you think that if I told her not to come that she'd just slink away and never try again?"

Damn. He had him there. "You should at least try."

"She knows damn near everyone in here from before she was out of diapers. Nothing is going to happen to her without many people standing up for her. She also doesn't show it, but she knows how to take care of herself."

"Knowing some self-defense moves won't stop a professional fighter."

"No, but the mace on her keychain would go a long way." Rich arched a brow at him, daring him to argue that point.

"Help me get out of these. I want to leave."

Rich nodded and opened the door, letting the trainer in. "You know these walls are thin and this room echoes."

Chad snarled at him as he walked away. That meant everyone in the hallway had heard them arguing. Again.

It was time to get out of here. Maybe he was done fighting for a while. She would probably forget about wanting to write about him if she didn't have him there to remind her.

Would he forget about her though? Unlikely. Dammit.

The next thought only questioned how bad it would be if he agreed to her article. He was tired of arguing with her and wanted the woman back from before he knew she was a reporter and wanted to write about him.

"Chad!" someone called as he left the locker room.

"Can I help you?" he asked as he turned to face the voice.

A man in a tan trench coat and a sweater-vest was flagging him down, pen and paper in hand.

"My name is John. I wanted to see if you had a quote I could get for the paper?"

This must be the colleague Kendall had mentioned. He looked like an asshole. "No."

"Come on, man. If I don't get this, my boss will have my ass."

"Yours?" Chad folded his arms and stared the man down. "Pretty sure it's Kendall writing this series."

"Women don't know shit about sports. You know I could do it better."

"Do I? You look like you've never been to a match before and probably know a hell of a lot less than a boxer's daughter."

"At least I'd have a chance at understanding. That's more than I can say for her. Genetics doesn't give her knowledge. She's better off painting her nails and minding her business than being here."

The messed-up part was that he'd been thinking similarly just a few minutes ago, that she shouldn't be here. Now, hearing someone else say it, it pissed him off. That also meant he had to admit he was wrong.

"Not a fucking chance. I'll talk to Kendall only, and I'll let your boss know both of you were here harassing me tonight." Chad let the threat hang, hoping it would send the man off.

John only stood a little taller. "You have no control over the press. I could take photos in public and post them without a release. Quotes would be nice, but they are far from necessary," he threatened.

"Do it and watch me sue your little paper into the ground. Might want to do your homework next time before you come in here threatening people you don't know."

Chapter Sixteen

Kendall skipped the next fight. She was tired of fighting with Chad, so she had focused on an article about her dad and another about Hugh.

It was enough to pacify her boss for now. Robert had made it clear that she wasn't off the hook on an article about Chad but had relented over the fact that her work was good enough to hold off on it for now.

Those two articles came with photos and were to be featured in Saturday's sports section. It was a big deal, and she wasn't taking it lightly, but she knew she'd have to come up with something better to keep Robert at bay.

John, for his part, hadn't spoken another word to her since the fight. She figured he had heard her arguing with Chad and was waiting for the right time to tattle on her like the child he acted like. She wasn't complaining though. She had no desire to chat with the man.

Sindee, on the other hand, had struck up a great conversation with Hugh and had been with him every day since. Kendall was happy for her, but she couldn't lie—she felt some jealousy that Sindee came to a fight only once and had gotten the guy.

Not that she wanted Chad to take her on a date, or hang out. She just needed the article, or so she had tried to convince herself. It was hopeless though. She knew she wanted him in both ways and had lost her shot at either.

At the fight tonight, she wasn't going to approach him. She'd made up her mind that she was done trying. For the last few days, she'd tried to get her dad to tell her Chad's last name so she could at least find out more about him for her own personal reasons, but he'd remained tightlipped on the subject, and she had given up.

Once again, Sindee was accompanying her to the fight, and this time Hugh was driving both of them. Her latest plan was to see if Hugh would let her follow his fights instead. She didn't know if he'd go for it, having already done one article, and it was a bit of a further drive to his home gym, but she could make it work.

"Oh my God, you're stressing me out. Would you quit pacing?" Sindee said, cutting off her thoughts.

"Sorry," she told her sheepishly and took a seat on the couch.

"I know you're stressed, but girl, lighten up a little."

"It's not your job on the line here," she snapped.

"I told you, just ask Hugh instead. I'm sure he'll go for it."

"I plan to. I just feel bad having to explain that Robert might not let the articles run."

"He'll understand," Sindee assured her. "Oh, he's here." She stood up and smoothed out her dress. "Do I look okay?"

Kendall gave her friend a smile. "You look amazing, as always."

They both headed out to meet Hugh and ride over to the fight. She briefly wondered how upset she was going to be that she didn't take her own car, but she let it slide. She was committed to staying to the end of all the fights tonight, and she'd just need to deal with Chad being in one of them.

The fights were getting more and more popular, and Tommy had teased the idea of charging admission as the crowd grew. She'd encouraged it. Why not make a little money off it?

He'd said he was still considering it, and she'd heard nothing else since. He was right though. The crowds were getting bigger. They were almost too late to grab decent seats as they shuffled in behind the growing crowd.

There were maybe a hundred people in attendance, but by comparison to the first one she'd been to, this was huge. Hopefully Chad wasn't upset over the growing interest.

She pushed that thought away. Who cared if he was? Not her. Nope, not one bit.

"Kiddo!" her dad yelled, making his way over to them.

"Hi, Dad." She stood up from her seat and gave him a hug.

"You staying the whole night?" he asked.

"She is. I drove them here," Hugh answered for her.

"Glad to hear it." Dad grinned. "I've got to head back, but make sure you say bye before you head out this time."

Kendall groaned. He'd been in the hallway by the locker rooms when she'd stormed out from arguing with Chad last week. That had been just a little humiliating.

She shrugged. "I'll do my best."

"We'll make sure of it," Sindee added, gesturing to her and Hugh.

"I knew I could count on someone." On a laugh, her dad walked away.

"Are you going to have me home by midnight too, before my carriage turns into a pumpkin?" Kendall looked at Sindee sarcastically.

"I think curfew is a bit later than that on the weekends. I mean, times have changed a little," Sindee teased back.

Hugh's laughter roared out as he slapped his knee. "You two are a mess. Do I need to sit between you to stop the bickering?"

Kendall laughed and stuck her tongue out at Sindee who pretended to be insulted. She then pointed a finger at Kendall, holding it about an inch from her shoulder. "I'm not touching you," she teased.

"Dad," Kendall whined, looking up at Hugh.

"Nope, I changed my mind. I don't want to be involved." He folded his arms and leaned back in his chair.

Kendall and Sindee shared a laugh before settling back as the first fighters were brought out. There were only two fights tonight. It amazed her that there were enough fighters around to even have fights once a week, but there were always new faces.

"Excuse me. Coming through."

Kendall's head whipped around as she heard Chad's voice heading her way. They locked eyes for a second before she turned her attention back to the fighters being introduced. There was no way he was headed toward her, so there was no point in watching him.

"Kendall," Chad said, finally reaching her.

"I'm not here to bother you tonight," she told him without looking at him.

"Kendall," he said again, his voice telling her to look at him.

"What?" she huffed.

"Hey, sit down!" someone from behind him yelled at Chad for being in their way.

"Sorry." He gave a polite wave and bent down so his lips were by her ear. "I'll do the interview," he told her.

The feeling of his breath on her sent shivers through her body before she registered the words. "Wait, what?"

"One interview. I want to approve the article before and after you send it to the editor, and that includes the photos."

Kendall nodded and swallowed. She wanted to ask so many questions but didn't want to disrupt whatever had happened to make things go her way. "I, umm, let me get my card." She shuffled in her seat, her legs brushing up against his as she did.

"Tonight," Chad told her. "After the fight, I'll meet you outside the locker room, and we can go get something to eat." He stood up and made his way back out of the row they were in.

"What was that?" Sindee asked.

"He, umm, said he'd do the interview." Kendall sat there, stunned.

"That's great news! Act like it!" Sindee told her and then turned to Hugh to tell him what was going on.

"I don't know why he agreed," Kendall said.

"Don't question it. Maybe he wants to hang out with you again." Sindee nudged her with her elbow.

"He wants to do it tonight, after the fights. He said we'd get food." Panicking now, she turned to Sindee. "I should have listened when you told me to get more ready. Oh my God, I look like I belong at the gym, not like I'm a journalist or on a date."

"Calm down. He sought you out, remember? I don't think you're doing anything wrong. Besides, I don't look like a journalist either—at least, not according to John."

A nervous giggle bubbled out of Kendall. "I certainly don't want to look like him."

"Here's some lip gloss because I know you have absolutely nothing in that purse. Put this on, and it'll all be better."

Kendall rolled her eyes in earnest this time but did what she was told. Something was better than nothing to make her look at least a little more feminine and a little less like she was headed for a workout.

Chapter Seventeen

C had was nervous as he took his time getting ready after the fight. He even showered in the locker room, something he never did, preferring his own shower to a shared one.

He hadn't seen Kendall in a week, and as soon as Rich said she was there tonight, he had slipped out to talk to her. It had been a long week, and he still wasn't sure this was the best decision, but he was going for it anyway.

His image consultant hadn't been happy with the idea of the article overall but said it wouldn't hurt. She had then let him know that her job with him was finished. He had rolled his eyes, agreed with her, and had sent her final payment yesterday.

He hadn't gone into this decision lightly though. He had a contract for Kendall courtesy of his lawyer that made sure he got the final say in the article. He had also opened up to the board about what he'd been doing, and though a few people had been shocked, no one had anything negative to say.

So, he'd decided he was going to give her the exclusive on him and exactly who he was, no more hiding. She hadn't been wrong when she'd called him a coward, but he was doing this to move forward with her, not because of that.

He'd taken a long look over the last week at his life and how he wanted to move forward. He still didn't know if he wanted to do anything more than local fights, but he had decided he no longer cared if anyone knew who he was.

Then it had only been a matter of telling Kendall. The John guy had pissed him off last week too, straight-up sexism always did, and the dude didn't even bother to hide it.

He took one last look in the mirror and let himself out into the hallway.

"You better act right," Hugh told him with a grin as he walked up.

"Sorry, umm, I rode here with Hugh and Sindee, so I wanted to make sure that you were okay with me riding with you before they left. If not, they can take me back to my car, and I can meet you wherever." Kendall's words were rushed, her nerves showing through.

He reached out and rested his hand on her shoulder. "I had assumed you would ride with me, so it's fine." He turned to Sindee and Hugh, sticking out his hand to Sindee. "I'm Chad. Nice to meet you."

She giggled before shaking his hand. "I know who you are. I'm Sindee, best friend."

Chad laughed and shook his head. "Some best friend you are," he told Kendall. "You're letting her go out with this guy?" pointing at Hugh.

"I know. I did try to warn her, but it was a hard battle," Kendall joked, and he was grateful to have broken some of the tension.

"We're going to head out. You two kids have a good time." Sindee waved.

"You guys too," Chad called as they walked away. "Shall we?" he asked Kendall.

She nodded, and he let her lead the way out of the gym and into the parking lot.

He didn't have a plan on where to go, so after a bit of debate, they agreed on getting some food and heading back to her place. She made it clear that she wasn't dressed for anything other than takeout, although he had no concerns with her tight-fitting light blue leggings and matching bra with a sheer shirt over top.

Takeout acquired, Chad drove them back to her place and parked just in time to wave at Sindee and Hugh as Sindee got into her own car.

"We got picked up from my place," Kendall explained.

"Ah," he said, not sure what else to say. "You get your keys out, and I'll carry the food." Chad got out and reached into the backseat for the takeout containers.

He followed her to her door, hesitating before he walked in. "Look, if you want to change, I can wait and we can actually go out."

"No, I'm good. This is better," Kendall assured him as she closed the door behind him.

"So, how do you want to do this?" he asked.

"We can talk as we eat."

"Sounds good to me. I just have one thing to settle with you first." He pulled the contract out from where he'd been carrying it rolled up in his pocket. "This assures that I get final say, nothing else."

She nodded, taking it and sitting at the table with her food. Kendall looked it over before getting up.

He worried for a moment that she was going to yell at him and kick him out, but it was everything she had promised before when she'd asked him to do the interview. She returned a moment later with a pen in hand and signed the paper before passing it back to him.

"I would have made sure without the contract," she told him.

"I believe you, but I can't risk it."

"Okay, so how about you tell me why you started fighting."

Chad picked at his food as he told her about his past and everything that led up to his decision to go to Rich for more training. He left in the image consultant and everything, giving her a full picture of who he had been.

She took no notes as he talked, which left him concerned, and he told her so. She promised she would remember, and he let it go. It was on her to make the article good.

Her jaw dropped as he explained who, exactly, he was and why he had made sure no one knew. His company was worth billions of dollars, and he didn't need the world knowing what he did.

She kept the interview casual, asking him questions here and there, but mostly listening to what he was telling her as she ate. He appreciated the informal nature of everything. It made it easier for him to talk to her.

As the interview wrapped up, he carried their takeout boxes to the trash, and Kendall stood up, asking him one more question.

"Why did you agree to this?" She tilted her head as though she was trying to work out a puzzle in him.

"I'm sick and tired of fighting with you. That guy John sought me out after you and I argued the last time and was a complete asshole. So, I gave it more thought and found that I couldn't stop thinking about you." He closed the distance between them and brought his hands up to her cheeks. "Tell me right now if this isn't what you want."

"I need you to kiss me more than I need my next breath," she whispered against his lips.

He felt the same way, and that was all he needed to hear. Lifting her up, he set her on the counter and covered her lips with his own. She tasted like heaven, and he knew right then that he'd never get enough of her.

She wrapped her arms around his neck as she held him to her. He poured all he had into the kiss, hoping she wanted more than this as he rocked his hips against hers.

Kendall threw her head back on a moan as he moved his lips to her neck. Sweeter and sweeter she tasted, and he was drowning in her murmurs of pleasure.

"Wrap your legs around me," he told her and picked her up off the counter.

He made his way down the short hall to her bedroom. He used his foot to push the door open wide before placing her on the bed. Kendall leaned back and watched as he pulled his shirt over his head and tossed it on the ground.

She licked her lips and he nearly lost it right then and there. Before he could tell her what he wanted, she started to undress from her spot on the bed as she continued to watch him.

He dropped his shorts and boxers before remembering to grab his wallet for a condom. Thank God he'd thought to put some in there, since he never carried them with him anymore, having recently been in a self-imposed dry spell while he trained..

As he stood back up, Kendall was shucking off the last of her clothes, and he feasted his eyes on her naked body on display there for him. That he was a lucky man was all he could think.

He rolled the condom on before bending over her on the bed and planting a kiss on her lips. He craved more of her as he slid down her body, feasting on her breasts. His hands wandered up and down her sides as he took one pert nipple into his mouth.

Kendall cried out and dug her hands into his hair, holding him to her. He changed positions and lavished his attention on the other breast as he slid his hands down between them, finding her ready for him.

"You're so fucking wet," he told her.

"I've been waiting for this for weeks," she confessed as she thrust her hips up toward his hand.

He'd been waiting too, and as much as he wanted to take his time, there was no way. This was going to be hard and quick. He covered her mouth once more with his as he thrust into her fully in one go.

She moaned against his mouth as her nails dug into his back. He broke the kiss and raised himself up as he worked his hand over her clit, rubbing it as she continued to writhe beneath him.

"Chad!" she screamed as her body spasmed around his.

Using his elbows to stop himself from falling all the way on top of her, he followed her over the cliff, riding the wave of his own pleasure.

She gave a whimper as he moved away to rid himself of the condom. He chuckled as he did and then returned to her. Pulling back the covers on one side, he lifted her up once more and set her down on the sheets before pulling the covers back up.

"Stay," she said softly.

He debated it for a moment, but in the end, the bed was too tempting. Climbing in next to her, he pulled her close before drifting to sleep.

Chapter Eighteen

Kendall stretched as she came awake. She was sore in the best ways possible and couldn't help the grin that split her face. Last night had been amazing and everything she'd expected it would be between them—explosive.

She reached out, finding the bed next to her cold. Sad at his loss, she lingered in the covers a while longer before finally getting up.

After a shower, she pulled out her computer and wrote the story that had been plaguing her for weeks. She wrote of his struggle to accept himself and how he'd finally found it through fighting.

Several hours later, she came up for air, only to realize she still hadn't eaten or gotten dressed. This was the way it was for her when she was into a story. It was the reason she'd never gotten a pet—she couldn't remember to feed herself most days.

Shutting her laptop, she realized that despite everything that had happened yesterday, she had no way to tell Chad it was done or to send it to him to review other than calling and he probably wouldn't answer. She'd just have to make her way to the gym to tell him, then.

Grinning and still feeling the effects of their night, she got ready and headed out. Her stomach reminded her, again, that she needed to eat with its loud growl. She stopped at Grady's first and ordered her usual burger and fries.

"Someone is in a good mood," Grady said as he brought her food out. "Things finally work out with Chad?"

"How could you possibly know that?"

Grady laughed. "I told you, I know everything."

"I want your secrets," she teased.

"I told you, it's magic."

She laughed. He'd been telling her the same thing her whole life. "I'm an adult now, so your magic line isn't going to work on me."

He waved her off. "But can I assume that I am right, then?"

Kendall just grinned back and popped a few fries into her mouth. "A lady never tells."

"Good for you, kiddo." He shook his head as he walked away.

She finished up and paid for her food, after the obligatory argument with Grady about whether or not she could, and headed to the gym. She arrived at the same time as her dad who greeted her in the parking lot.

"How'd it go last night?" he asked.

"How'd what go?" she deflected.

"Right, because he didn't leave the locker room to come talk to you right before the fight. And he definitely didn't shower at the gym before meeting you in the hallway. And you definitely didn't leave with him last night."

Red-faced, she ducked her head. "It went well. I have the article for him, and I just came by to tell him."

"Oh sure, because I must be blind," he teased and held the door open for her.

Chad was already working out, so she took a seat by Tommy and chatted about the fights. Tommy was more excited about them than anyone else she'd talked to, and he loved the articles.

He swore it was her articles that were bringing more people into the gym and to the fights. They'd had several new membership signups since the articles started.

Her day continued to look up. It was nice when the unexpected side effect of the article was positive for other people.

Chad approached and said, "We need to talk."

"Sure. I have the article whenever you want me to send it over. That's what I came to tell you."

He pulled out a business card and handed it to her as he led her away from everyone to a corner of the gym that was empty. "We can't do what we did again," he told her.

She felt herself deflate as he spoke. He only wanted one night with her. She choked back the tears as she looked up at him. "You're serious? I thought we had something between us," she replied, keeping her voice low.

"It's not smart for either of us to get involved."

"Why's that?" she challenged.

"My email is on the card. Send the article over, and I'll take a look at it as soon as I can. Come to the next fight if you need photos, and that's it. We can't do this."

She wanted to argue, wanted to throw a fit and make him talk to her, but she let him walk away. Without another word to anyone, she left the gym and went home.

The second she got there, she pulled out her laptop and sent the article to the email address that was on the card. She included no preamble to it, just a line that it was for his review, and then closed her computer.

How had a day that had started out so well ended so miserably? Why had the universe given her everything she wanted and then snatched it all away? The self-pity train was miserable, but she was on it now.

Sindee had called her several times, but Kendall wasn't in the mood to chat. She sat on her couch, curled up in a blanket with a pint of ice cream, watching chick flicks. She didn't even want to get in her bed because it smelled like him, and that both pissed her off and made her cry.

Tomorrow she'd pull herself together. She'd wash the sheets and rid her house of him and his smell and move on. Tonight she'd wallow in her own misery for a little while longer.

She pushed Play on the next movie and dug into her ice cream just as someone knocked on her door. Her heart leapt as she thought it could be Chad coming to confess what an idiot he was.

Sindee let herself in, took one look at Kendall, and grabbed a spoon. "Tell me what happened and how I can hurt him," she said as she climbed under the blanket with Kendall.

"There's nothing to do. He doesn't want more than last night, and that's his choice. We never discussed anything about it being more. It just is what it is."

"Oh, honey." Sindee hugged her. "Where's the fight I know you have in you?"

"I'm tired of fighting."

"Be tired then, and take a rest, but you love him. You can't just let him walk away because he's scared."

Love him? Did she? She tried to think on that only to come up with the same answer each time. She was screwed.

Chapter Nineteen

He felt like shit. The worst part about it was that he knew why, and he couldn't do anything about it.

Rich was his friend and his coach, and Chad had gone off and slept with his daughter, which made him a piece of shit. She deserved better than him, anyway.

He was reviewing the photos from the fight last night that Kendall had sent over. Even her emails were cold, and it was nothing less than he deserved.

She'd gotten some great photos, he had to admit. He expected some messy ones because she was mad at him, but he should've known she wouldn't be like that. Not only did she not have it in her, but she would be professional for work.

He hadn't intended to tell her like that or to just break it off without at least telling her why, but the more he looked at her, the more he knew he'd cave if he tried to talk to her. Instead, he'd been an asshole, and she'd let him walk away.

It had been almost a week, and he still felt like an asshole, and he missed her. She needed to stay mad at him, though, so she'd stay gone.

Rich had also barely spoken to him and then taken two days off, something that he'd never done the whole time Chad had been working with him. The man had never stayed away from the gym —until now.

That meant he knew. There was no other reason for it. Even though Chad had tried to stop Rich from finding out and being mad at him, he'd found out anyway and was now even madder at him because he'd hurt Kendall.

His life was a fucking mess, and there was no one to blame but himself. He texted Rich and let him know he wouldn't be back at the gym until Monday. He needed a break but blamed it on work instead.

It wasn't a lie. He intended to bury himself in contracts and documents until he couldn't see straight and then go home and go to bed. Thankfully, he had no fight this weekend.

Wondering if Kendall was going to attend the one that was happening made him feel sick, so he needed to focus on these contracts. Focus on anything that wasn't her or related to her.

He sent off the approval of all the photos and the final approval of the article before moving the emails to a folder that wasn't his inbox where he'd see them every time he opened it before digging in to work.

Half an hour later, his phone chimed with a text from Hugh.

Hugh: What the fuck did you do?

Chad: What needed to be done.

Hugh: Based on what? Sindee said she's never seen Kendall look this bad.

That stabbed at him, knowing he was the reason.

Chad: I can't change it, I wish I could. This is for the best.

Hugh: You're an idiot.

Chad didn't bother to reply. Hugh was right.

Standing up and stretching, he decided this wasn't working and left the office. He headed back to his apartment, somewhere he'd never invited Kendall, despite wanting to.

"Dammit!" He slammed his fist into the steering wheel. Thinking about where she hadn't been wasn't solving the problem of thinking about her.

He wished he could say he regretted sleeping with her, but that had been the best night of his life. When she asked him to stay, and he'd held her close all night, everything had felt perfect.

Then he'd woken up the next morning to a text from Rich, and reality had set back in. It wasn't just about the two of them. His decision to be with Kendall was going to have rippling effects throughout his life.

Even the article itself was going to affect him. Everyone that didn't know who he was would know now, and it could change how fights happened and who challenged him.

He'd had a ton of time to think and had finally decided what he wanted to do with his life going forward. The company didn't take up much of his time, and while he enjoyed training and the fights, it wasn't something he wanted to take any further.

Chad called his lawyer and asked him to meet at his apartment. He had a plan but needed to know how to proceed with it. This, at least, would show he wasn't a complete asshole. Maybe Kendall would write an article about it.

He shook his head. No, she wouldn't. He wouldn't want to either if he was her.

Getting out at his apartment, he headed inside and started making notes of all the things he wanted to do. That way he'd have some sort of plan when his lawyer got there.

After writing several pages of notes, he answered the door when his lawyer arrived.

He'd known him for a while but had skirted the edge of friendship with him. They could joke together but that was the limit, normally. His suit was freshly pressed, as always, and fitted him perfectly like he'd been born into it.

"What's going on?" he asked.

"I decided what I really want to do, and I need your help to make it happen."

"Tell me what it is."

Chad nodded and went through his notes, discussing every detail he'd thought about for the community outreach program he wanted to start. This wasn't going to be aimed at kids in an income bracket, but instead, it was to help kids who were bullied learn patience and some fighting skills.

"This is really great. It will look good from a public-relations standpoint too. Do you have any idea where you want to do it?"

Chad shook his head. "I hadn't thought about a location, but I do want Rich onboard. He loves kids, and he's great at teaching patience in a way that makes you have to listen to him, want to listen to him."

"Shit, can I take classes?"

Chad laughed. "I'm going to give him a call and see if he's willing to meet."

"Is there a reason he wouldn't be?"

"Oh, I just slept with his daughter and then broke it off."

His jaw dropped as Chad hit Send on the phone call. It took a few rings, but eventually Rich picked up.

"Hey Rich. I know I'm probably the last person you want to hear from, but I have a proposition for you, and I'd really appreciate it if you would hear me out," Chad rushed out, worried Rich would hang up at any moment.

"I'm listening" was all he said.

"I have this idea of creating a safe place for kids to come to learn to fight. Kids that wouldn't otherwise have the opportunity to learn to defend themselves. I want to make it accessible and teach more than fighting."

"How does that involve me?" Rich asked.

The fact that he was still on the line much less asking questions was a win, and Chad would take it.

"I was thinking the way you taught me patience and the breathing techniques would be great here for the kids. Even if you don't want to teach them, you could give advice on how to teach them?" As far as sales pitches went, he knew it was lacking. "I'm here meeting with my lawyer and was thinking if you had time, you could stop by and help us with the ideas?"

Rich's sigh was loud through the phone. "I'll be over shortly. This doesn't change anything between us right now. This is only because I think it's a good cause."

"Understood. And thank you."

He felt like an ass to even be asking him to help, but there was no one else that could give him this knowledge. He knew that when he was looking for a coach, there was no one like Rich, and his talents couldn't be denied.

Less than an hour later, they were all sitting around Chad's dining table, making a list of things that needed to happen. Rich had been more excited once Chad explained exactly what he was looking to do and how he wanted Rich to help.

"No offense, but I'm done with coaching after you. It's exhausting. I want to relax when I go to the gym or just enjoy the fights instead of being involved."

"Don't worry, I won't keep you much longer. I will finish out every fight that I've already agreed to, but then I will just be keeping in shape, maybe a spar or two, but I'm out as well."

As his lawyer left, Rich lingered. "I don't know what happened, and I'm not going to pry. It's not my place, but I hope you sort it out."

He didn't have to say he was talking about Kendall for Chad to know. He wanted to ask more and find out how she was doing outside a random text from Hugh, but he didn't. It would only serve to make him feel worse no matter how she was doing.

Rich left, and Chad headed back to his table and cleaned up all the notes. It would take a while to get started, and Rich had given them a few ideas of empty locations they could look into, but he was excited to have a purpose in life again.

If he could keep any kid from feeling even a fraction of what he'd felt growing up, then he'd know he'd accomplished something.

Chapter Twenty

On the day the article ran, Kendall couldn't take it any longer. She bought a few copies and then headed to the gym. If he wasn't there, she'd take it as a sign and leave it alone. If he was, then he was going to get a piece of her mind.

If only for closure, she needed to talk to him. She needed to know why when they had finally found their way to each other, he'd changed his mind. And despite being a strong, independent woman, who normally didn't care what people, especially men, thought of her, she couldn't help but wonder if she had done something wrong.

Her dad didn't mention him at all, and she was both grateful for that and annoyed by it. Hugh had offered to spar with him in her defense, but she'd declined; she needed to talk to him and then move past this on her own. He and Sindee were officially a couple now, and it was absolutely adorable.

While she now avoided most of Chad's fights, she had attended a few she knew he wouldn't be fighting in. She'd even written a few more articles about Hugh.

Robert had loved her piece on Chad, and it had cemented her place at the paper, even as she questioned if this was truly what she wanted to do. John had been pissed, so naturally, she had been elated —in the moment anyway.

She was toying with the idea of doing something more meaningful with her life and had told Sindee about it. She had smiled like she was keeping a secret but wouldn't tell Kendall what it was.

For now, she was back to writing sports and looking for her next story. If she could help it, it wouldn't be about anything to do with boxing, or MMA, or fighting at all. Maybe she'd turn in the article on the trades from the soccer team again and see if she could get an exclusive there.

She entered the gym with a stack of papers and walked over to Tommy.

"Have you seen it?" she asked.

"I've been waiting on you to get here. You promised to bring it to me, so I didn't get a paper this morning."

"Here you go." She handed him a newspaper.

Tommy flipped through the pages until he reached her article. He took his time reading it, and she knew when he'd gotten to the parts that were about him by the small smile that spread across his face.

She'd purposely not looked anywhere else in the gym yet, but she knew Chad was there. She could sense him looking at her.

"Girl, I think this is the best work you've ever done."

She smiled at the praise before helping him pin it to the wall. She hadn't looked at the spread until now. It had come out nice, even if it did mean she was staring at a picture of Chad.

"Tommy, I need to let you know something," she leaned over the desk to tell him.

"What's that, girl?" he asked.

"I'm about to cause a scene."

A big smile spread across his face. "It's about damn time you did too."

She gave him a conspiratorial wink and walked away, leaving the stack of papers on his desk. There was only one person she wanted to speak to right now, and he was currently pretending she wasn't there and that he hadn't noticed her.

"We need to talk," she said as she stood next to the weight bench he was using.

"There's nothing to talk about," he told her, placing the weight bar back on the rack.

"Fine. If you don't want to talk, then you can listen."

"Stop, Kendall." She could see the panic on his face as he tried to prevent her from speaking.

"I'll stop when I'm good and ready. I'm tired of dancing around and not having the real conversation about what happened between us."

"Fine," he relented, "but not there. Let's go to the locker room."

"No, here's good. Everyone listens at the locker room door anyway." She glared at him.

"Kendall, come on. Your dad is standing right there."

A lightbulb went off in her head. That was his issue? "You think he doesn't already know? You think everyone in this gym doesn't already know?" She laughed. "Everyone knows, and if they didn't, they thought they did."

It wasn't a thrilling thought for her to know that everyone knew her love life was a hot mess, but there was no denying they all did. That meant they knew his business too.

Wide-eyed, he stared over her shoulder. Kendall turned to see her dad grinning at the two of them.

"Best of luck, man," he told Chad before turning to the growing crowd. "That's it, nothing to see here. Go on and explore the basement for a few minutes, and let these two kids try to sort out their lives."

Groans came from some of the men, but everyone went along. She waited until everyone had left before turning back to Chad.

"I don't understand what happened. I need you to tell me what was so wrong about that night." Now she figured it was probably a misguided sense of loyalty to her dad, but she wanted to be sure.

"Kendall, you did nothing wrong."

"Then what is it?"

"I owe your dad a lot, and I didn't want him to think... I don't know." He stood up and looked down at her. "I don't know what's wrong with me. You didn't do a damn thing wrong."

"I don't care if you're a fighter, you know? I mean, it definitely wasn't on my short list of careers for a boyfriend, but it doesn't matter to me. It doesn't matter to my dad either."

"What if I'm done fighting?" he asked.

"What?"

"I have a few more fights that I've already agreed to, and then I'm mostly done. I still want to train and maybe spar, but I'm done. I have bigger plans."

"Wh-what plans?" she asked, confused now.

"I'm starting a nonprofit to help kids that are bullied learn to cope. Your dad is helping me."

Sindee must already have known, and this was the secret she was keeping. Damn, it sucked to be around so many people who were so good at keeping a secret.

"You have to know that it doesn't matter to me either way. It really doesn't. I think this is great, but if you do that, or fight, or just go back to working at your company full time, that's got nothing to do with why I'm falling in love with you."

Chad smiled for the first time since she'd looked his way today. "Say it again," he urged.

"I can't help it. I've fallen in love with you."

"I love you too, Kendall." He picked her up and spun her around as he kissed her. "Never stop fighting me when I'm an idiot. These past few weeks have been miserable without seeing you at all."

Cheers interrupted their moment as everyone from the basement filed back into the gym. Her dad walked straight for them.

"I'm a firm believer in letting people figure it out for themselves, but you two had me worried." All smiles, he turned to Chad. "Next time you think I'm going to have a problem with something, then come to me. If I had an issue with you and Kendall, I would have made that clear from the start."

"Yes, sir," Chad answered.

"And you." He turned back to Kendall. "Sometimes all a guy needs is a fighting chance."

"Sometimes he needs a kick in the butt," she joked.

"As long as you're around to give it to me when I need it." Chad pulled her tighter to him. "I missed you."

"I missed you too." She rose up and kissed him in front of everyone. "There's no getting rid of me now."

"Thank God."

Epilogue

Epilogue – One Year Later
Sindee's Sanctuary Article

Dear Readers,
    As you know, I have touched on sports here and there, and while this does approach that topic, I think this situation is a little different. After a year in the making, Hard Shell finally opened this week. Catering to all ages, people can learn self-defense, coping mechanisms, and boxing all in one place. Hard Shell's goal is to help people that are bullied or need help finding their way.

    The gym opening was attended by its founders, Chad, Kendall (our very own sports reporter), and Rich, who, rumor has it, have been there every day. They worked hard and it should be celebrated, especially for such a great cause.

    Now for the even better part. Tuesday night after the gym's opening celebration, our dear Kendall was proposed to by Chad, and she accepted! I'm freaking out for her and can't wait to report on all things wedding related here for you.

    Kendall's father, Rich, who was part of the inspiration behind

Hard Shell, was overcome with joy and had to be consoled by his friends, who were attending. The bride-to-be was all smiles after the proposal and still is, almost a week later.

Proud husband-to-be, Chad, has reportedly started planning a lavish honeymoon. I am hoping the couple slow down and have the wedding we all know they deserve, but I'll be happy for them even if they get married tomorrow.

Regardless of timing, you know I will have the inside scoop and have been promised the first wedding photos to publish! I know we are all looking forward to those. Kendall will continue to be the sports reporter here, and I hope that if you see her at any games, you take the time to congratulate her.

It means a lot to me that some of you have reached out to check on my own relationship and wonder how it's going. Hugh and I are doing great, even when I'm not reporting on it. We've settled into that wonderfully boring part of a relationship where we are both enjoying time with each other even if we don't go anywhere, but I hope to have more news for you soon!

Hugh's fights are usually local, and I attend each one I can. If anyone is interested in coming out, Kendall will have the schedule posted today. I encourage you to come out and support our local fighters when you get a chance. They are truly amazing to watch.

Lastly, since Kendall hasn't reported on it, Chad will not be returning to the ring professionally, He says, "I accomplished what I needed to and proved something to myself along the way. My focus now is helping others do the same." So there you have it. There will be no more chances to see him fight. Sorry, ladies.

As always, I hope you have a lovely week and will keep you all posted on any updates. If you're free Saturday, the farmer's market will be hosting local musicians throughout the day next Saturday. If you see me, feel free to say hi!

Always wishing you the best,
Sindee

Liked it?

Please consider leaving a review on the retailer you bought this book from!

Authors thrive on reviews

Also please recommend on BookBub if you enjoyed it. Thank you for reading and please look ahead at sneak peaks of other stories by me.

Keep In touch with Toni Denise

Follow Toni Denise on Social Media!
Facebook
Instagram
Twitter
And Sign up for her Newsletter to find out about awesome games
and new releases.
Sign up here!

Also by Toni Denise

Learn More or get buy links for any of these books at my author website:

tonidenisebooks.com

Westbeach Series:

Old Friends

On the Run

One Last Chance

Out of Time

Series Boxset

Finding Love Series:

Engaged to Her Neighbor

Married to the Playboy

Falling for Her Fake Husband

Short and Steamy Duet:

The Wedding Date

The Wedding Ruse

Stone Twins Duet:

Please Stay

Don't Leave

(Don't Leave is included in the "Mine This Winter" collection available Dec 1, 2022)

Billionaire Blind Dates:

Owen (free with newsletter sign up)

Jake

Evan

Standalone:

Fighting Chance

Owen

Don't miss the prequel novella, to the Billionaire Blind Dates Series, Owen's story, exclusively available in my Newsletter for free!

Owen is a man who always knows and gets what he wants, but when he goes to the bar to grab a nightcap, he gets more than he bargained for. He meets a woman who's unlike any he's ever known but saying goodbye to bachelorhood will take some convincing.

Jenna isn't thrilled with the idea of going on a blind date, but a deal is a deal, so she shows up. She meets a great guy, who saves her from what would've been a disastrous date. Unfortunately, she never hears from him again.

Even though, the unplanned date goes well, Owen has a big decision to make. Is Jenna the one who will make him rethink bachelorhood?

Find out what happens in the prequel novella to the Billionaire Blind Date Series!

To read the full story, sign up for my newsletter!
www.tonidenisebooks.com

For a preview, turn the page!

Owen
Chapter 1

Owen stepped into The Striped Keg bar and looked around. The dim lighting was a stark contrast to the well-lit street he had just come in from.

Men and women chatted throughout the room, most standing at tables with a few lining the bar. He came here specifically to avoid too much conversation. Plus, as it was across town, no one recognized him.

They could if they looked hard enough, but few ever did, and that was what he wanted. A drink and some peace.

Walking around the old wooden bar, he took a seat at the far end and waited for the bartender to notice him. It had been a disastrous week, one he'd like to forget, and here where he blended in, it helped.

"What can I get ya?" the bartender asked.

He handed over his card. "Start a tab. I have a ride home, didn't drive here. Scotch."

He always made it a point to let the bartender know he wasn't driving. It helped make sure he wasn't cut off before he was done for the night.

"All right." With a curt nod the bartender walked away.

Owen

"Excuse me?" A pretty blonde in a black dress approached him. "Are you Kyle?"

Owen shook his head.

"Damn. Mind if I sit here?" she asked as she set her small purse on the bar and sat down without waiting for an answer. "Why I let my sister set me up on some stupid blind date with a guy name Kyle of all things, I'll never know. Then he's not even here on time? Way to set the tone."

As much as he didn't want to be, he had to admit he was intrigued by the plain-speaking woman next to him. She didn't even seem to care if anyone was listening to her monologue, just kept on going.

The bartender brought Owen's drink over and turned to the woman.

"A beer, please. Whatever's on tap is fine."

"Add it to my tab," Owen said without thinking.

It was stupid. She was going to sit here now and keep talking to him and there went all hope for his night of peace.

"You don't have to do that," she told him as the bartender walked away.

"Looks like you could use a good break tonight, figured maybe it would cheer you up."

"I'm not going to sleep with you," she said boldly, causing Owen to choke on his first sip.

"What?"

"Just because you bought me a drink and my date didn't show, I'm not so grateful that I'll drop my panties for you tonight. I don't do one-night stands."

Owen couldn't hold back the bark of laughter that spilled out. "You're very blunt," he told her.

"No sense in not saying what you mean here in a dark bar with strangers. If you want, I can pay for my drink myself when he comes back with it."

"It's okay. I don't mind paying for it with nothing in return." He flashed his most charming smile at her. "I didn't intend to get anything for it as it was."

"Thank you."

Her drink showed up a moment later and he let the bartender know she was on his tab until he closed out.

"Why'd you think I was your date?"

"Wishful thinking, perhaps?" She shook her head at herself before turning back to him. "You were late getting here and your tie is the right color."

"My tie?" It was a light green, one he wore often, favoring the color.

"Yeah, he's supposed to be wearing a green tie. That's vague enough, but what shade of green? There's so many, and then so many men in here with green ties."

He nodded as he listened to her ramble on about ties. She was animated when she talked, and he found himself enjoying it and her company. Normally he carried the conversations but didn't feel the need to with her.

"Sorry," she said suddenly.

"For what?" He tilted his head, trying to figure out what happened.

"I always talk too much. It's a fault of mine and annoys people." She sipped her beer as though that was making it all better because she couldn't talk.

"Oddly enough, I was enjoying your speech on ties and the various colors of green."

"Liar," she said but then grinned up at him.

"I am in a position where I don't want to be the only one talking but I seem to always be doing just that. Having someone I don't need to pretend I want to do all the talking with is refreshing."

"Well, flattery will get you everywhere," she laughed. "Except my bed."

"Got it. Not sleeping together tonight."

She shook her head but laughed.

"Excuse me, are you Jenna?" A man in a poor-fitting suit stood next to her.

Still facing him, he could see the indecision on her face as she looked back at who had to be Kyle. He looked like a jerk and was definitely older than both of them.

Finally, she answered, "I am. Are you Kyle?"

He nodded and then didn't even bother to hide it as he checked her out from head to toe. "Must be my lucky night. You are stunning."

Owen rolled his eyes and sipped his scotch. This guy was going to get nowhere with her and he was interested in watching it happen.

"Sorry, if you were looking for a hookup, let me save you the time. I won't be sleeping with you for at least a few months, if you last that long."

Thank God he had already swallowed his drink or he would have choked on it again. Owen let a small smile sneak out as he watched Kyle try to decide what to say to that.

"Months?" Kyle asked, the shock evident on his face.

"At least three, maybe six," Jenna confirmed.

"Umm, well, I," Kyle stammered and pulled at his collar.

Taking pity on him, Owen jumped into the conversation. "Dude, just cut your losses and find a new bar and date."

Kyle seemed to just register his presence as his gaze slid to Owen. "I mean, it's not that we had to tonight, but like, that's a long time."

Owen just shook his head. "Go on."

Kyle seemed slightly relieved as he spun and disappeared into the crowded bar.

"You really should have let him sweat it out a bit longer."

"Couldn't. The man looked like he was going to pop before he ever managed a sentence."

"A pity he was only looking to get laid. I'm never letting my sister set me up again. Where'd she even meet him?"

Owen laughed. "He looks like a used car salesman, and not a very good one."

Jenna threw her head back and laughed. "God, yes. That's exactly it."

"Months, huh?' Owen arched an eyebrow at her.

"For him? Absolutely. If ever." She looked at her phone. "He's almost an hour late and was clearly checking me out before he decided if he wanted to have the date. It's going to be a no, bud."

"Bud?" Owen teased.

"He looks like he calls people bud."

He agreed and nodded. The man one hundred percent looked like he did. "Well, now that you have no date tonight, what are you going to do?"

"You're not my date?" Jenna fake pouted before giggling. "Don't look so horrified. I'm not trying to trap you."

"Not horrified, more curious," he answered simply. "So what was supposed to happen on this date?" Curious now, he found he wanted to keep the conversation going and know more about her.

"I assumed we'd chat over drinks and decide if we wanted a second date. Didn't really think about it that deep to be honest."

"What a crummy date," Owen said.

"I agree. I really should have just stayed home."

"Now, that I wouldn't have agreed with."

Just then Kyle walked by again. "Months," he muttered, shaking his head before turning into the crowd again.

"Dude's a creep," Owen observed. "Want to get out of here?" he asked her.

Jenna pinned him with a look that had him backpedaling.

"To get pizza. I swear. It's walking distance, too."

She stared at him for a moment, and he knew she was deciding whether to believe him or not before she nodded.

"Bartender!" Owen called. "I think we're ready to pay." So much for the tab he'd been planning to run up.

Jake

Billionaire Blind Dates Book 1

Five men form a bond over their mutual business opportunities and the trials of finding real love in a world of greed.

After Jake discovered his last girlfriend was in it only for his money, he has given up on dating, tired of being used. It's hard to find the right woman for him when everyone knows who he is and what's in his bank account. At poker night with his friends, they come up with a plan. They will all use the new blind date service offered in town where everything is done through an app and dinner dates are done in the dark with only minimal lighting to see if the pair hit things off. Each man gets to pick a person for the others to blind date, with just a few rules.

Lauren doesn't like rich men. Almost all the ones she's known seem to think that women should bow down to them since they have money. She's over it and would like to find a respectable man to date that doesn't have loads in the bank. Someone who, like her, just wants to live comfortably, not lavishly. She also hates being thrust into the media. When her boss's sister begs her to go on a blind date, she reluctantly agrees, thinking she will just get it over with to stop her from asking again.

Lauren and Jake hit things off immediately. How will Lauren react when she finds out who Jake is? How will Jake react when he finds out he's dating his friend's assistant?

Evan
Billionaire Blind Dates Book 2

Kayla knows a thing or two about making love connections. As the owner of Blind Date, a popular app and restaurant that creates a safe and completely dark environment to meet, date, and find love, she's successfully helped others find love, but she's never used it to find love for herself.

Evan is thrilled by the public's reaction and the revenue its generated. As a silent partner, he gets to reap his share of the benefits while staying completely out of the way. A friend found love with Blind Date, but Evan doesn't put much stock in finding it for himself. His friends, however, convince him to give it a shot. All he has to do is survive four dates, and if it doesn't work out, he can walk away.

After two disastrous dates, he's ready to back out of the deal, but he's not a quitter. Remarkably, the third date is a charm. Things go so well; it almost feels familiar. There's just something about date #3, but he can't figure out what.

When she suddenly stops replying, he's dumbfounded. He doesn't where he went wrong, so he seeks a woman's perspective from Kayla. Her reaction isn't what he expects and turns the whole blind dating concept on its head.

Evan

What happens when business partners realize there may be more to their partnership than meets the eye?

Find out in BILLIONAIRE BLIND DATES: EVAN

Sneak Peek

If you're interested in book with a little more suspense, read ahead for a preview of Old Friends, the first book in my Westbeach Romantic Suspense Series.

Old Friends

Sometimes a second chance can be the last chance.

Recently divorced, Kelly finds herself back in her hometown. Deciding that starting over is key, she and her son take to living a new life.

When a second chance with Mason, an old flame, ignites, Kelly is excited to feel love again.

But something is wrong. Someone is watching them, waiting to strike. Someone that knows them. Someone. . . close.

Not knowing who she can trust, Kelly is thrust into a life of fear and looking over her shoulder.

Where do you turn when the one person you thought you could trust might actually be the person you're running from?

A steamy romance novel with a moderate heat level.

Old Friends
Chapter 1

Taking in the scenery, Kelly wondered why she never came back to visit. Going home was hard, but it was only about a four-hour drive. She really should have come home before now. Taking the long road around the outside of town, the scenery alternated between trees so dense the automatic headlights came on in her car and open pastures with cows or horses in them. This time of year, everything was still bright green. It looked pretty, but she knew better; being late August, it was hot out there. Soon the brilliant green would give way to a wonder of colors as fall slowly crept in.

Turning the music down, she focused on the GPS and the last few miles of her trip. Traffic had started to pick up in the previous hour of her journey until she left the interstate. She was glad she had left earlier in the day; it was only about 4:00 p.m. now. A quick check of the back seat showed Hunter was waking up. For a seven-year-old, he wasn't a bad road-trip partner, but he had slept all but the first hour, when he ate most of the snacks. "Hey, Hunt, we're almost there. Are you excited?"

"Are we in a zoo?" Hunter sleepily asked.

Kelly took another look around, wondering why this was even a question. Cows. There were cows on both sides of the road. "No, baby, there are ranches around here that raise cows."

"So, I'll see the zoo every day?"

"Yes." Simpler to agree than to explain more as he wasn't awake yet. Besides, in all his seven years, he'd never seen the countryside, and Westbeach was about as opposite of DC as you could get.

As they made the last turn, the woods on either side were a welcome presence, adding shade to the last bit of the trip, which had been mostly on the sunny highway. She was going to have a sunglasses tan for sure. Finally pulling in to the driveway, Kelly breathed a sigh of relief to see her aunt and uncle already there and waiting for them.

The light blue house was one level and had a small new porch on the front. The wood was still white looking, so she could tell it hadn't been there long. The front yard was freshly cut, and there were trees on both sides of the property and behind it. A privacy fence, which also looked new, wrapped around the backyard. No neighbors could be seen unless you were in the road. *Wonder if I'll be able to sleep without the noise of the city?*

Aunt Mary was the first to come off the porch as Kelly parked the car. Mary, in her signature flower dress and floppy hat over her white hair, had always been able to style anything except herself. Her dresses were like something older ladies probably wore in the fifties. Gardening, cooking, shopping—same dresses; some things never changed. Bob, on the other hand, was a jeans and T-shirt man. Kelly could never remember Uncle Bob having hair—on his head or face. Much like Mary though, his style was the same no matter what he was doing. The only thing these two changed was the colors each day.

When Kelly stepped out of her car, Aunt Mary immediately wrapped her in a welcoming hug. "How are you doin', dear? How was the trip?"

"Let her get out of the car, Mary." Uncle Bob always sounded a tad sour but was a sweetheart underneath.

Old Friends

"I am, I am." Aunt Mary backed up and opened the back door for Hunter to climb out of the car. "Hunter! You've gotten so big!" Hunter grinned and stood tall at her praise. Mary ruffled his hair and proceeded to go to the trunk with Uncle Bob to get their bags. "Is this all you brought, honey?"

"For now. The rest is packed, and Dylan is supposed to send it this week, but we'll see if he remembers to let the movers in or not."

"Okay, let us know if you forgot anything." Aunt Mary smiled sadly at Kelly.

"You know I will." She plastered on a big smile to reassure everyone that she really was okay. Taking Hunter's hand, she turned and walked into the house.

When she walked in, the first thing she noticed was that the house was fully furnished; some things even looked new. A gray sofa in the living room faced a flat-screen TV with a small coffee table. Passing through the living room to the kitchen, she noticed there was a cherry-colored table for four with a bouquet of fresh flowers waiting for them. *Definitely Aunt Mary's idea.* And the smell—some version of every spice, but in a good way—was just like Bob and Mary's house. It was a welcoming scent, the smell of home.

Kelly walked down the hall of the modest one-story house, pulling her suitcase behind her. Three rooms, two bathrooms—per Mary's directions, hers was the last on the left. The room had a large queen-sized bed in the center with a gorgeous purple quilt and matching pillows on it. A dresser sat against the long wall with a mirror attached.

Checking all the doors, she discovered the closet was behind the open bedroom door, and against the wall was a master bath. A purple shower curtain hung already with silver bath mats. Aunt Mary really should have been an interior designer, and her remembering Kelly's favorite color just made it that much better.

Kelly had never been able to have everything decorated in her favorite color before, but now she could do her thing. Putting her bag down she took a deep breath; divorce wasn't going to be too bad if this was how it started. Coming back home wasn't all that bad, even if it did make her feel a little like a failure for her marriage not working.

There was no love lost in her marriage anyway. Dylan didn't even fight for custody of Hunter. He just let them go and agreed to everything—not that she had asked for much, just child support and custody. Dylan didn't even want weekends with Hunter. Kelly sighed as she looked in the mirror and pulled her hair into a ponytail before heading back out to the other three noisily chatting about cows in the dining room.

"Hunter tells me he's excited to see the zoo every day," Uncle Bob informed her with a laugh as he pulled Kelly up for a quick hug. Although pushing seventy, Bob was still a tall man. He was the exact opposite of Mary, who was shorter than Kelly by five inches, standing at five feet tall. The family had always joked that it was her hat that gave her an inch or two and that she genuinely was less than five feet. Mary had always laughed along as well, shushing everyone, but never argued it.

"Something tells me he'll eventually tire of it," Kelly said with a small laugh of her own.

"I stocked some essentials in the cabinets and fridge; wasn't sure what all you would need. We can go to dinner later, or you can come over and I'll cook." Aunt Mary always made sure everyone had eaten. If you weren't hungry, she was going to have you doing something until you were. "We are waiting on the handyman though. The disposal isn't working right now."

"No problem, and we can eat whatever is easiest for you tonight. Thank you guys again." Bending down, she hugged Aunt Mary again and gave her a kiss on the cheek. "I don't know what I would do without you guys here."

"Family helps family, dear." And that was all Aunt Mary was going to say about it. No thanks needed ever.

"I love you." Before either of them did more than tear up, Kelly changed the subject. "The handyman? Is that who redid the front porch? It looks nice."

"Yes, yes. Bob thought he was going to do it. Took the boards off and then decided it was too much for one old man, like I said." She cut a look at Bob, who decided not to say anything and continued to talk to Hunter. "Thankfully," Mary continued, "the handyman was able to get out here and get it done before you got here."

"Really?" Hunter shouted and jumped up from the table to run out the back door.

"I told him there was a swing set out there." Bob smiled and moved to follow Hunter out the door.

"He will never come inside again." Kelly laughed and moved to the window to see Hunter happily swinging while Uncle Bob looked on.

"Go unpack, and I'll wait right here for the doorbell," Mary said while shooing Kelly from the window. "He'll be fine."

"I know. I'll be in his room for now if you need me."

Wandering down the hall, Kelly opened the door across from her room and was pleased to find an office. Mary really had thought of everything. A small desk sat facing the window with a fancy-looking high-backed office chair, and she could see the entire backyard from there. A tall lamp in the corner would keep her from having to turn on the overhead light to see, and a ceiling fan was a nice addition. The room was painted a darker shade of blue, but it didn't seem to make the room feel smaller.

There was plenty of room left in there for her treadmill since there was no gym here that she knew of, and going for a run would be difficult with Hunter still home for the summer. Mary always knew what worked and what didn't without even trying. Kelly would be glad to get back to work in two weeks in her new office. Thankfully, her legal transcription was work from home, and they had been generous with her time off under the circumstances. She would have a pile of work when she got back to it though. It was going to be rough going back to work after all this time off. Thinking about her emails that she hadn't checked all day, she walked out of the room and closed the door.

Moving on, Kelly checked the room next to hers and saw a twin bed, some toys already set out for Hunter, and a large baseball poster on the wall across from her. Smiling, she walked over and touched it, amazed by the little things Bob and Mary had thought of to help Hunter adjust. She'd also bet money that there was no swing set here before Kelly decided to move in. Kelly heaved Hunter's suitcase on the bed and started to unpack and put away the clothes.

"I didn't pack hangers." Kelly let out a deep sigh. "If this is the worst part, I'm good, right?" Musing to herself, she walked down the hall to see if Mary wanted to go to the store. "Mary, are you interested in running to the—" Seeing a man in the kitchen, Kelly stopped midsentence.

"Kelly, this is Mason, the handyman. Mason, do you remember Kelly?"

"How could I forget?" Drying his hands off, he looked up, and Kelly stared into eyes she hadn't seen in twelve years. Mason Cole.

"Wow! How are you? It's been forever." Not sure what to do with herself, she leaned awkwardly against the wall, taking in this man who had been a teenager when she saw him last. Instead, here was this man with his dark brown hair and muscles she could see through his blue shirt. And those blue eyes... a woman could get lost in those eyes. He hadn't changed much other than getting older, like her she supposed. He was still as handsome as ever.

"How's the set working out?" Mason interrupted Kelly's assessment of him. Oh, that smile, crooked with one dimple on the right cheek. That smile could make women fall all over themselves to get a glimpse of it. Nope, that hadn't changed one bit.

"Hunter is already out there." Mary saved her from having to form an answer. Nothing could have prepared Kelly for seeing this man in her kitchen.

Swallowing down old feelings and trying to move forward, Kelly shifted to look out the window on the back door to see Hunter still outside playing. Taking it in for the first time, she noticed the back deck was only slightly above ground level, just one step up. *I need to get a table and chairs for out here, so I can work and watch Hunter play.* The yard was a fair size, plenty of room for Hunter to run around, and the start of the tree line had been fenced into the yard, giving him a shaded place to play. The swing set was a good size as well, containing two swings, a slide, and monkey bars on one end. Uncle Bob strolled from the deck to the yard, watching Hunter wear himself out. *At least he'll sleep tonight, even after that long nap in the car.*

"What did you need, dear?" Aunt Mary asked.

"Oh, I didn't pack hangers and was wondering where the closest store was?" She focused on Mary, anything to not stare at this too-hot-to-be-here man in the kitchen.

"That would still be Gersham's down on Main Street. I have to head there to order the part for your disposal if you'd like a ride?" Of course, it was Mason who answered. And a ride, really? Lord knew she wanted to go for a ride. Wait, where had that thought come from? How unlike her; must be the nerves.

"I don't want to impose. I can head down there later."

"No imposing at all. Grab your bag and hop in the truck." Interesting how the words he chose said he made the decision, but the tone made it clear it was still her call.

Grabbing her bag, she let Hunter know she would be right back. For all he cared though, he was still enthralled with the swings and slide out back. After hugging Aunt Mary, she walked out to the dark blue Dodge Ram sitting in her driveway. Mason was standing by the truck and opened the door for her. He waited until she had settled before closing it. *What am I supposed to say now? What do I do?* Placing her bag in her lap, she sat still as he climbed in and backed out the driveway. Not much was said on the way to the store.

Staring out the passenger window, she watched the scenery. Everything seemed the same, and yet it all seemed so different at the same time. When they got to the store, they went their separate ways after Mason pointed her in the right direction. She grabbed several packs of hangers and headed toward the checkout. Mason was already standing there putting in an order for whatever part it was he needed.

As she approached, a shiver ran down her spine. Kelly felt like someone was watching her. Looking around, she didn't see anyone else in the store besides Mason and the clerk. Still, she picked up her pace, unable to shake the creepy feeling. She set the hangers on the counter, continuing to look around while waiting for them to finish. *You're losing it. No one is in here, just the empty store getting you creeped out.*

Needing a distraction, she watched the interaction going on at the register. The woman was practically hanging on Mason's every word like she was super interested in garbage disposals. Kelly rolled her eyes. When she looked up again, Mason winked at her. She had been caught. Completely distracted from the creepy feeling, she now had a new one—full-on embarrassment.

Part ordered and hangers paid for, they walked back to the truck again. Mason took the awkward bags of hangers and opened her door for her. While Kelly buckled in, he put the bags in the back seat, then shut her door and got in.

"Didn't like her much, did you?"

Kelly felt the heat creep up her face. He wasn't going to ignore her eye roll. "It wasn't that. More of a disbelief type of thing." *There, that makes me sound less rude for not liking someone I don't even know and positively not jealous.*

"Nope, it's been a while, but you still can't hide anything. It's all over your face," he teased.

Kelly put her hand to her heart and leaned toward Mason, doing an exaggerated impersonation of the busty clerk. "Oh, please tell me more about garbage disposals." She batted her lashes. "I just don't know what I would do without you having come in today, Mason." Kelly laughed and sat back right in the seat.

"Pretty good impression actually. Now you know why I didn't want to go to the store alone." Mason cut her a sly look but laughed as well. After a moment, they both fell into a companionable silence for the rest of the trip. Pulling up, Mason stopped her from opening the door with a hand on her shoulder. "It's good to see you and have you home again, even if it's not under the best of circumstances."

"Thank you. I'm glad to be home. No love lost in the reason for my coming home, so no worries. I'm glad I got to see you."

"If you need anything while you're here, let me give you my number. Your aunt and uncle call when something needs to be done in one of their rentals. Most of your new home has been newly renovated though; they really went all out to make it right for you. Oh, and I'll let Bob know when the part comes in. She said Tuesday, but when I pick it up will depend on when I can get someone to go to the store with me." Mason laughed again.

"I noticed. The porch looks great, and the swing set too. If you let me know when the part is ready, I can run in and pick it up, and then you can avoid the store altogether." Kelly winked at him. "You can just let me know. Let me find a paper, and I'll give you my number." She dug through her bag and came up with a crayon and a receipt. Blushing again at how much of a mess she must seem, she wrote her number down and handed it to him. Saying their goodbyes, she hopped out of the truck and went inside with a smile on her face.

#

Kelly Marie Holstead, he didn't know she would be there today. He could have sworn it was tomorrow that Mary said she would get here. Pulling into his own driveway, he smiled as he remembered Kelly's reaction to Darlene, the clerk at Gersham's. Just like the old Kelly would have done, she let loose with that cute little eye roll. Heading inside, he greeted Shep, his aging yellow lab, with a pat on the head. Shep followed him through the house, waiting to be let outside. Grabbing a beer from the fridge, Mason opened the back door and went out to the deck, Shep in tow.

Checking his phone, he texted Nate, his brother and business partner, about the disposal and the part needed. He pulled Kelly's crayon-written number out of his pocket and plugged it into his phone. *Should I text her now, so she has my number? Is it too soon?*

After deciding to just program the number in and debate it later, his thoughts wandered to the day he had. After a rough morning with two young guys late to work, again, he was frustrated and cranky when he remembered he was supposed to check on Kelly's disposal today. When he pulled up, he was in no mood for small talk with Mary but had resigned himself to it. Then he noticed another car in the driveway.

Kelly apparently hadn't been expecting him. He wasn't entirely expecting her either. He hadn't seen her in almost twelve years, since they were seventeen and about to graduate high school. That summer was some of the best memories he had though. Kelly was his best friend, but when they went to college in different states, they had slowly lost touch. It was one of his biggest regrets. He and Kelly had shared everything—sometimes too much, but he could always tell her anything, and she, him. He knew Kelly had gotten married right after she graduated college, and that was about it.

She still looked as good as ever, a more mature woman and no longer the body of a teenager, but time had been kind to her. Her blonde hair had been pulled back, but it was more than shoulder length and had some highlights. Her body though, she looked like she took care of herself; he could see her defined leg muscles under her shorts. Her curves were more significant than he remembered. She wore no makeup, probably not something she usually did, but no reason to get dolled up for a road trip to move. He liked the no makeup look though, no pretending, nothing to hide.

Just then his phone went off, pulling him out of his thoughts as they headed in the wrong direction. Texting Nate back, he got up, adjusted his pants, and Shep followed him in the door. Nate was going to give him a hard time about seeing Kelly, and about venturing into Gersham's when he knew Darlene would be working. He wasn't kidding; he had taken Kelly as a bit of a buffer. Darlene always shamelessly threw herself at him, but she'd limit it to flirting if there was someone else in the store. The woman never took the hint that he wasn't interested, even though he had tried to let her down gently many times before. Now he just avoided the place when he knew she was working.

Time to make dinner. Pulling out the chicken, he got started on cooking. *Wonder if she still cooks as well as she used to?* What the hell was he doing, thinking about her so much? It had only been a few minutes, and nothing had even happened to make him feel so much about her. She hadn't thrown herself at him like most women, so what was it?

Finishing up dinner, he carried it to the living room. Watching TV would distract his wayward thoughts.

#

He waited in his car with the lights off until Mason had finally left Kelly's house. He had watched her from the back of the store as she searched hangers. He couldn't believe she had been home just a few hours and was already back with Mason. How had that happened? Had to be her meddling aunt. He had been watching the house for the past week waiting for her arrival and would meet her again soon. She was supposed to come back after she finished school, and like a fool, he had expected her to, but no, she went and got married and hadn't come back at all.

He had followed her online for a long time and had made sure she found out about her husband's cheating. Chuckling to himself, he remembered how easy that had been. He had just pretended to be the secretary's doctor and called their house phone looking for the father of the baby. Of course, Kelly had answered. Then he "accidentally" spilled the news of the baby to her. He had gotten her home now. She hadn't been happy in her marriage anyway, so he didn't feel bad. This time, she would be his, and neither Mason nor anything else was going to stand in his way. He carefully put away his phone, excited to have new photos of her on it, and headed home.

www.ingramcontent.com/pod-product-compliance
Lightning Source LLC
Chambersburg PA
CBHW050859180626
46814CB00007B/2793